THE LOVE HEALER

A.K. LEIGH

Serenade Publishing

To all the amazing trauma survivors: may self-love be your guide on the road to trauma recovery.

PROLOGUE

NOVEMBER, present year

Neoma's Journal
Entry #159

I'm here. Sitting on the assigned seats on the promenade overlooking Sydney Harbour. It's getting dark and strangers are strolling around; some are getting close to me, and I feel fine about that. How different from twelve months ago! Lights from a couple of boats are blinking at me from across the water, almost like they are in on some shared secret. Is that a good sign or a bad one? Even though I've done several breathing and grounding exercises to prepare myself, I still feel tight (in my chest) and nauseous (below my diaphragm). I know it's a positive step for me to be this conscious of the way my body feels, but that doesn't mean my mind accepts it.

Thank goodness I've gotten into the habit of taking my journal everywhere. Writing in it gives me a sense of security.

Probably because it reminds me of Emerson. Ah, writing his name makes me feel more nervous. Oh, God. What if he doesn't come? No. He will. I know it sounds crazy–though both Mum and Cara said they trusted my intuition–but this is the first time I have felt so certain about anything in a long time. My body feels it, too. It's buzzing with the possibilities. Yes, the nausea and tightness are lingering, but that's nerves, and I'd say most people would feel nervous in this situation. Wouldn't they?

I mean, it's possible he won't come.

I need to take a break.

My head is starting to spin ...

Okay. That's better. I've taken more slow breaths, given my arms a shake, and swayed my upper body from side to side to shift as much anxiety as I can (got some funny looks, but who cares?). Now I can refocus and move the jumbled words from my mind, through my fingers, and onto the page. Unedited. That's still hard. Even after a year of practice. In some ways, the time has passed as fast as a blink; in other ways, it's lagged as slow as Cara's scooter on a good day. Speaking of slowness, how much longer until he gets here? My watch says 7pm. He shouldn't be far away.

Aah! What am I doing? This is insane. It's been a year. He's semi-famous now. Gorgeous models must be throwing themselves at him every day. He's not going to come back for me.

So what if he doesn't? Ha! I shrugged at that question. If he doesn't show, then Emerson's not the only fish in Sydney Harbour, is he? I'll be fine, whatever happens. I have been fine this past year. Better than I was for the six months before I met him. It will be his loss more than mine. I'm smiling now because I can feel the truth of that in my body. The tightness has gone.

Only a touch of anxious nausea remains. I really have come a long way. My confidence is back. Finally. When I think about the events that brought me here, it's hard to believe I am the same woman who first met Emerson ...

CHAPTER ONE

Neoma

SEPTEMBER, the previous year.

A buzzing sound startled me from my restless sleep and half-nightmares. I jolted upright, trying to orient myself as my heart rate spiked. What was the sound? I narrowed my focus. Had it been part of the nightmare? Was I imagining things? Wouldn't be the first time …

It took another moment to realise I knew the sound. I exhaled in relief. Nothing to get worked up about or over-analyse. *Just. My. Phone.* I peered around as the disorientation subsided. Everything was familiar. Safe. *I'm still in Cara's guest bedroom. Not the apartment.* My heart rate slowed as I reached for the phone on my bedside table. The screen alerts showed I'd missed a call. From my mother. I pressed my lips together to contain my frustration. At least she hadn't left a message. The phone buzzed in my hand. *Nope.* She'd left a message. Why was I surprised? She hadn't honoured any of my boundaries or requests for seven months. I rolled my eyes, then set the phone back down. Cara would delete the message for me if I asked her.

At the thought, the familiar voice of my best friend called out, 'You awake, sweetie?'

'Yeah. I'm up.' My voice sounded choked, either from the lack of sleep or my mother's phone call. Probably both?

'Breakfast is ready.'

'Thanks, Car, but I'm not hungry.'

I knew what was coming next. This had become our routine: Cara asking me to come and eat with her, me making an excuse not to. Some mornings she caved and some mornings, I did. It wasn't that I didn't want to eat; it was more that eating with other people around had lost its appeal. Most often, I snacked alone throughout the day instead of having meals with others.

'You have to eat.'

I replied the same way I always did, 'I'll eat later. Could you leave it on the counter for me, please?'

A pause made me think Cara had caved and left, but in a gentle tone, she said, 'Sweetie …' *Oh, great.* Whenever she said it like that, a lecture was coming. Sure enough, she added, 'You can't go on like this. It's been six months.'

Longer. My thirtieth birthday had been six months, two weeks, and three days ago. But who was counting? My chest squeezed with anxiety as a subtle meaning behind her words came to me.

I blurted out, 'I know I've overstayed my welcome. Sorry, Car. I'll go back to …'

My voice cracked as a sharp image flashed through my mind. I blinked and shook my head to force the image away, and found I couldn't voice the words I'd intended. *My apartment.* I had realised for a couple of months now that the apartment didn't feel like home anymore. But I'd been stuck in a kind of limbo. Not wanting to go back, but not moving forward, either. What was I going to do? I couldn't return, and Cara clearly didn't want me to stay with her any longer.

As if she'd read my mind, my best friend said, 'You know you can stay here for as long as you need. That's not a problem. Can you open the door so we can talk properly?'

I pulled the twisted covers from around my body, hopped out of bed, and walked to the door. I unlocked it and cracked it open enough to see Cara's face. The concern that wrinkled her forehead made me look down. I hated affecting her this way. It wasn't fair.

'Look at me.'

I obeyed as Cara looked me up and down. A half frown marred the edges of her mouth when she saw I was in the same pyjamas I'd been wearing for a month. I was a disappointment. That's what the look on her face said. I thought the same when I caught the odd, accidental glimpse in the bathroom mirror. I had been too stupid, taken one too many risks, didn't know how to keep my loud mouth shut, and now I was bringing her down with me. Why did she bother sticking around to help me?

I drew in a deep breath, the way everyone seemed to

suggest you should at moments of stress. It didn't help me relax.

'I'm trying to respect your journey here, Neo, but I'm worried about you. You need to try *something* to help you move on.'

Oh-oh. I knew that tone. She was up to something. I was pretty sure I knew what that something was.

Pre-empting her, I said, 'If this is about seeing another psychologist, I'm not interested. I hate all that talking. You know that.'

'That's why I found someone you won't have to talk to.'

Huh? That was a first. In the months I'd been living with her, Cara had booked me in to see two different psychologists, both of whom I'd refused to see for a second session because of their focus on what they referred to as 'talk therapy.' I'd left their offices feeling worse than before I'd gone.

I put my hand on my hip as I gave her a scrutinising look. 'What does that mean?'

'You don't have to talk about anything you don't want to talk about.'

I noticed she hadn't directly answered my question but had given me enough information to make me ask a follow-up question. 'What do I do? Sit and stare at them?'

'Not exactly.'

I caught something in the way she'd said it. She was being wishy-washy. Why? What wasn't she saying? She only did this when she knew I wouldn't like what was coming.

'Please let this go. Whoever she is, I'm not talking to her.'

How much more of 'read this self-help book, it'll help' and 'try this CBT exercise, it'll help' and 'tell me more, it'll help' was I supposed to endure?

I started to turn away when Cara blurted, 'He doesn't use talk therapy.'

He.

I paused as that pronoun sunk into my brain, then double-checked, 'Did you say "he"?'

She nodded. 'He's an ex-psychologist, for the army, or something. He gave that up to focus on the less mainstream healing therapies.'

Less mainstream healing therapies. What the heck did that mean? She was talking in riddles. 'You have to start speaking a language I understand.'

Cara grinned. Something I hadn't seen her do with me the entire time I'd been living with her. A gentle nostalgia washed over me. I missed this, missed Cara, more than I'd realised.

She said, 'I knew you were still in there.'

I looked down, because I knew what she meant and disagreed. The woman I'd been was long gone. She touched my arm. Without conscious control, my body pulled away the instant she made contact. I frowned, hating that reflexive reaction to my best friend. She would never hurt me, but my brain didn't seem to comprehend that.

I glanced at her and said, 'Sorry.'

She shook her head. 'Don't be. You haven't done anything wrong.'

Except, I had. Otherwise, I wouldn't be in this situation. Neither would Cara.

My best friend continued, dragging me from my too-familiar self-criticism, 'He's helped a lot of women with similar situations to yours.'

'I'm happy for them, but you know therapy hasn't helped me.'

'He uses a completely different therapy model. Less formal, unorthodox, and adjusted to the individual.'

I scoffed. 'He sounds like even more of a quack than the others.'

'It's helping people. *He's* helping people. I've researched him.'

I hesitated. What excuse would stop this conversation? A reasonable excuse came to me. 'It'll be too expensive for me long term.'

I hadn't worked in months, was living off my savings, and wasn't sure what my long-term career options were going to be. Costly therapy was the last thing I needed to worry about.

She shook her head. 'He's more affordable than the others you've seen, and he has flexible payment options, including sponsored places for those who can't afford it. Besides, I've paid for the first session already.' I attempted to object, scrambling to find another excuse, but she talked over me, 'Please, Neo, do this for me if not for yourself. Just one session, then I won't bug you about it again.'

I raised an eyebrow, hopeful. 'Ever?'

'Ever.' Why did I get the feeling she was crossing her fingers? Still, if it got her to stop hassling me, it might be worth it. She carried on before I could reply, 'You spend so much time alone in your room, your panic attacks are getting worse. And the nightmares. I heard you again last night. They--'

She stopped what she'd been about to say when I looked away, refusing to see the worry in her eyes that made me feel even crappier about myself than I already did.

'I'm worried about you. Please agree to the session.' She had raised her voice halfway through the last sentence, exasperated as much as worried about me now.

I understood. I had become exasperated with myself so often these past months. This person I had become was pathetic. All because of one incident that had lasted ten minutes. Why couldn't I snap out of it and move on? Something needed to change. I knew that, but nothing had worked so far. I'd tried 'letting it go' like the new-age gurus suggested and my once-regular meditation practice had only provided an open space where the memories could float back in. Ignoring had worked until it hadn't. As had working overtime. I was now on a forced leave of absence--after an incident at work that I couldn't fully recall the details of--and had no clue how long my job would be on hold. Even though the psychologists had been Cara's idea, I'd tried my best when I'd seen them. I'd even read some of the book suggestions, from both Cara and the counsellors, and attempted many of the set Cognitive Behavioural Therapy exercises. But none of it had helped. It took everything within me just to get out of bed every day. I wanted to 'get past it' so I could 'live my life'--yes, all the clichés and then some--but keeping to myself and staying in my bedroom were the only methods that had provided an ounce of emotional relief. Was I supposed to give that up for something that didn't help?

Cara begged, 'Please, Neo. Even if there's a small chance it could help, isn't it worth it?'

A small chance it could help. Those words sunk into my mind. How long did I want to keep living the way I had been? The books I'd read and the counsellors I'd been to hadn't helped, but they'd all agreed on one significant point: reaching a place of growth and thriving after a traumatic experience was possible. Did I want to try to thrive rather than survive? Was the smallest chance of this counsellor helping worth it? *Am I worth it?* That unbidden question echoed deep inside me, insulting the confident woman I had been. I knew what I had to do.

I looked up and asked, 'What's his number?'

Cara grinned in victory and handed a slip of paper over to me. My sneaky friend. She knew I would cave and ask for the number.

When I took the paper, she said, 'I've already set up an appointment time.'

Of course she had paid for *and* booked the session already. That sounded exactly like my direct and organised best friend. I sighed, resigned to the fact, then read the writing on the paper. *Thursday, 10am.*

After reading the name Cara had written under the appointment day and time, I looked up and quipped, 'His name is Emerson Novak? Sounds like a dick.'

'That dick is going to help you feel better. I'm sure of it.'

Judging by the look that crossed her face, we both

caught the accidental double meaning of her words. She grinned, but when she saw I wasn't smiling, she frowned. In the past, I would have laughed with her. But that was who I had been before. I was grateful when Cara didn't comment further. She was great like that. Yes, she could be pushy, like she was right now, but she also seemed to know when to pull back. I'd always envied her innate sense of discernment. Maybe if I'd had that gift, I wouldn't have gotten myself into trouble. I threw that conclusion aside to refocus. Me getting 'help' was one point Cara had consistently pushed for. The pessimistic side of me that had come to the fore these past months said it was because she was sick of living with my sorry ass. Another side knew she was looking out for me, the way a best friend should.

I tried to align with that side as I said, 'I will be there.'

'Thank you, sweetie.'

With another victorious smile, Cara walked out and closed my bedroom door behind her.

From outside the door, she called out, 'I'll leave your breakfast on the kitchen counter before I leave. Try to eat some of it.'

'Okay. Thank you.'

In the silence, my mind went over the conversation. Somehow, it had morphed from me eating breakfast to an appointment with a not-shrink. My best friend had a talent. She should work for the police. I paused at the thought. Hadn't Cara said this Emerson person was ex-army? A touch of interest flirted with my brain as it lingered on the word 'ex'––why had he left the army? Had he been kicked out? *Hmm.* I wasn't sure I cared enough to get stuck on those questions. After all, Emerson Novak was another counsellor I would never see again. Right? It took about one more second before the overanalysing that had become a habit threw more questions at me. What were his mental health qualifications? What kind of therapy didn't use talking? Was I supposed to sit and stare at him the entire time? I frowned. What had I agreed to? More importantly, would it end up being yet another decision I regretted months later?

CHAPTER TWO

Emerson

I KNEW what I would find before I even opened the wine fridge. *Empty.* I closed my eyes and puffed out a breath in irritation at myself. Why hadn't I thought to stock up yesterday? *When would you have done it?* My private practice had taken off thanks to the tireless efforts of my manager, Jack, so I'd ended up accepting an emergency client after-hours. The day and evening had gotten away from me. I'd fallen to bed in an exhausted heap. After slamming the wine fridge's door, I realised I'd have to go out. There was no way I could attempt my ritual without alcohol. Every year before now, I'd planned the ritual to perfection so I would have two days off to carry it out. Looked like this year was going to be different.

Under my breath, I growled, 'Fucking fantastic.'

I marched to my ensuite bathroom to check on everything else I would need. If I had to make a second trip out, I might implode. I opened the mirrored medicine cabinet built into the ensuite's wall and peered inside. *Sleeping pills for tonight.* Check. *Cologne for tomorrow night.* Check. *Condoms for tomorrow night.* Check. Alcohol was the only missing item. I closed the medicine cabinet and caught my reflection in the mirror. Two days' worth of stubble dotted my jaw. I touched the stubble with my thumb and index finger. Should I shave? Was the effort worth it? I shrugged. Women these days didn't seem to care about facial hair. I'd wait to see how I felt later.

When I grabbed my wallet, phone, and keys, I hesitated at the front door. What if I went out and was recognised? Now that my public profile was getting media attention, it might be best to have a makeshift disguise. The possible alarmist headlines––*Unorthodox in more than just his methods: Emerson Novak spotted buying armfuls of booze alone*––could harm my growing positive reputation in the field of unorthodox trauma therapy. Not only that; others would get involved.

First, my parents. *Ugh.* Mum would be 'disappointed' and Dad would offer a lecture whether or not I wanted it. Sil, the personal psychologist assigned by the army after *the incident*, would remind me of his thoughts on the ritual, 'It is a negative coping mechanism.' Jack, who had worked the past eighteen months to build up my reputation, would bark at me, 'You advocate against the use of coping mechanisms, so why were you photographed coming out of a Bottle-O all liquored up?'

None of them understood. How could they? I mean, as a trauma expert, I understood these views. But ... the way my stomach lurched told me I did not want to skip the ritual. I'd organised it to help me through this difficult time of year. I'd organised it with care. Hadn't I? I lingered on the question, then nodded when another niggle in my stomach convinced me I *had* to go out. The ritual helped me. Which meant I needed a disguise. As I glanced around, my gaze stopped on the dark sunglasses and cap I left on the hall stand near the front door. *That would work well.*

Chapter Three

Neoma

I FORCED a stop to the cascading questions. No point in brooding over them when I didn't really want answers. After running my fingers through my hair and sweeping it up into a rough bun, with enough fringe to cover some of my face and eyes, I walked towards the kitchen. The scent of the scrambled eggs on toast Cara had left drifted to my nose. My stomach grumbled. How long since I'd eaten? I didn't bother with cutlery. Instead, I scooped up the toast in my hand, took a big bite, and chewed. Hints of Himalayan pink salt, freshly ground pepper, melted Swiss cheese, and garden-fresh chives rolled over my tastebuds and down my throat. *Mmm. So good.* I sighed from the simple pleasure. I'd forgotten how well Cara could cook. Most often, she left cereal, muesli and yoghurt, or vegemite toast for my breakfast. This extra effort was probably her way of making up for the psychologist swindle she'd played on me. I took another bite. *Yum.* Almost worth the appointment to get her to cook like this. *You can cook too, remember?* My best friend and I had cooked together often. We'd been known in our circle of other friends as the people who could host both a glamorous dinner party and a casual barbecue. I hadn't boiled water in six months.

The thought made me realise how thirsty I was. I put the rest of the toast back on the plate and went to the fridge. A sticky note had been stuck to the fridge door. In Cara's handwriting, I read: *we're out of bottled water. Could you get some if you have the chance today?* I exhaled, reading what wasn't as blatant as the words she'd written. This was something Cara had started recently; setting minor tasks to get me out of the house. There was never any pressure to carry them out. Cara didn't get angry with me if I ignored the notes, which was most of the time. She would call later to check if I'd done it, then do it herself if I hadn't. It wasn't that I was trying to be nasty or lazy, it was the thought of going out, the effort I would need to make. *Yuck.*

I ripped the note from the fridge, ready to bin it with the eggs that now sat in my stomach like thick balls of wool. Halfway to the bin, I hesitated. Cara had looked after me these past months. Yes, I wasn't mooching off her financially thanks to my savings--which would dry up in a couple of months--but emotionally, I was bleeding her dry. She'd been patient and understanding, tried to help me, and made me delicious eggs for breakfast. Yet, I couldn't go out and get her a couple of bottles of water when she asked so little from me. What kind of friend was I?

I glanced down at my pyjamas. Could I be bothered changing? If I hurried, I could change back into them the instant I returned, then spend the rest of the day in bed. On the plus side, I could grab a chocolate bar, too. The thought of milky, sugary gooeyness was too strong to ignore. Decided, I turned to the kitchen sink, tilted my face underneath the kitchen tap and guzzled the drink I'd needed. Some of the water splashed onto my face. I wiped it away. *That's my face washed today.*

Two minutes later, I walked into the garage wearing a pair of track pants, long-sleeved top, mid-thigh length knit vest, and loafers. All black. Great colour for hiding dirt and blending into the background. Thank goodness Cara had a scooter––from her first ever job as a delivery girl––because she let me use it when she had her car. My car was still at my old apartment. Public transport was not my favourite option: too many strangers jostling up against you. From experience, I knew the sensation of being pressed against could trigger anxiety and unpleasant memories. Hence, one of the reasons I preferred to keep physical distance between myself and others. I wanted to avoid a potential panic attack in public. The handful of other times they'd happened in public had been humiliating and disorienting.

I pulled on the helmet she kept with the gold-coloured scooter, started it up, and pressed the button to open the garage doors. When I pulled onto the driveway, I noticed the thick, grey clouds hovering above me in the sky. *Hope it doesn't rain.* I drove off, with the clouds seeming to

follow my journey. A short time later, I shuffled inside
the local chain supermarket. As I made my way to the
bottled water aisle, I kept my eyes down and sidestepped
away from people who passed too close. Once I was in
the right aisle, I paused at the shelves and tried to
remember the dimensions of the scooter's back storage
box. How much bottled water would fit in? A pack of
twelve or six small bottles? Better to go smaller than I
thought, right? Otherwise, I'd be balancing the water on
my lap. Annoying.

'Six pack it is.'

I grabbed a couple of chocolate bars along with the
water. Thankfully, the line to pay was short, so I was out
in a couple of minutes. Stuffing the sweets into my vest
pockets, I adjusted the pack of water bottles until I had an
even distribution of weight in my arms.

I took a step around the corner of the shops, then
stopped to check how many people were around, to
determine my best route to the scooter. Which way would
prevent accidental bumping the most? An unexpected
beam of sunlight hit my eye, making me squint and turn
my face--*no rain today after all.* With the turning action, I
noticed someone walking towards the Bottle-O a short
distance from me. *A man.* My heart jumped to alertness as
I narrowed my attention on him. The man wore dark
sunglasses and a cap, which added an intriguing aura of
mystique around him. *Wonder who he is?* The shock of that
thought made me drop the water. I hadn't wondered
about a male stranger in a non 'is he a threat' way for
months.

The man turned in my direction at the sound caused

from the impact of the bottles. At first, he looked confused, then he saw the bottles.

'Let me get that for you.' He'd retrieved the water before I could respond. 'They don't look damaged.'

I nodded stupidly and must have taken the water from him because I became aware of a renewed weight in my arms. He stared down at me, as if waiting for a response. My turn to speak. *Say something!*

'Thanks.' That's what I think I said.

He nodded, flashed another friendly smile, then said, 'Have a nice day.'

When he walked off, I scolded myself. Hadn't I learned anything about strange men? I stormed off towards the direction of the scooter. During my ride home, with the occasional burst of sunlight hitting me through the once-again grey sky, the interaction with the man I'd nick-named *Water Guy* replayed. It hadn't felt like he was 'putting on' the politeness so he could 'get something in return.' He hadn't asked for my number or done anything resembling sleazy. Or creepy. No come on. No subtle double meanings. Nothing. All he'd done was help. Then he'd left me alone and carried on with his day. As far as I could tell, he hadn't even ogled me. I glanced down at myself. The black trackpants, baggy long-sleeved top, and vest were hardly the stuff of male fantasies. I'd barely finger-combed my hair and washed my face before leaving the house. What man would want me like *this*? For the first time in months, that thought did not bring comfort.

CHAPTER FOUR

Emerson

I HEARD MYSELF GROAN. The sleeping tablets I'd taken late last night to prepare for today's planned ritual were wearing off. Waking consciousness was approaching, but the day didn't need to know that yet, did it? My usual plan involved sleeping as much of this day away as possible.

Once it became impossible to pretend I was still asleep, I'd drink a glass of whiskey to reactivate the drug lingering in my system, then sleep again. I knew the risks associated with this practice––using alcohol to top up the effects of the sleeping pill circulating in my blood could make my heart rate drop so low I might not wake up–– but the ritual helped take the edge off the anniversary day. It was the only thing that worked. I'd wake up again once night fell. Then I'd get my body moving in as many distracting ways as possible until it was all over.

Besides, I was mitigating the risk involved. I had my watch set up to monitor my pulse and heart rate and to alert the ambulance if either of those became too low. This wasn't a dangerous coping mechanism, binge spree, or addiction like the ones I often saw in my clients. I took safety precautions. Unlike them. The thought made me check the settings on my watch. As I did, I noted a couple of messages had come through earlier that morning. Mum and dad's message was more-or-less the same as Sil's: *Let me know if you need to talk.* The words made me sigh. I appreciated my parents' and ex-psychologist's concern, but if I returned a message, they would assume I wanted to talk. Previous years had taught me that lesson.

It was bad enough with my parents, but Silvester Clearwater was an eminent army psychologist whose techniques had helped many ex-army trauma survivors. He'd been assigned to me after the incident. Even though I'd officially called off our therapy sessions a while ago, I respected him and his knowledge, so I'd asked him to be my mentor. Since the organisations that regulate psychologists have guidelines around changes in relationship between therapists and former clients, we'd negotiated a new set of boundaries and responsibilities between us. We'd also had to address the inherent unequal power dynamics. Under our new agreement, I would take on some of Sil's overflow clients pro-bono. In exchange, Sil would check in once a month for mentor-related tasks, and also offer therapy for me at this time of year. Except, I didn't need therapy. I was fine. Ignoring the messages, I went back to checking my watch. *All set.*

The fact I had a ritual proved even more that I was

operating from logic, not emotion. My psychologist-trained brain decided that was the best time to pop in for an unbidden comment. *You can't ignore this anniversary. It* will *catch up to you.* I exhaled in frustration. Why couldn't that part of me shut up sometimes? I *wasn't* ignoring the anniversary. I was approaching it from a logical standpoint. Knowing it would be difficult, I prepared. I didn't react; I planned. Nothing wrong with that. Structure and planning were positive coping mechanisms. Getting stuck in emotional triggers and engaging in negative coping mechanisms didn't help you recover from a traumatic event. So, I did the opposite. There was no room for emotion on this day. *If you're so sure, why haven't you told Sil you're still engaging in the ritual?* I shoved the unspoken question away. Evidence-based practice. That's what this was. The ritual had helped me navigate the anniversary just fine these last seven years.

No …

Eight years.

Today marked *eight* years. I'd been twenty-five, a bright-eyed, optimistic, and thoroughly naïve psychology graduate. The memory sent a chill down my spine. The fact I was aware of the sensation told me I was more awake than I wanted. Maybe it was time for the bottle? I forced my eyes to open. The bright sunlight slipping through the gaps in my curtains tried to trick me into believing it would be a cheerful day.

'Yeah, right.'

The sound of my sleep-tightened voice startled me. I hadn't intended to scoff out loud. But there was only one way to improve this day: get through it as fast as possible, with as many distractions as possible.

I glanced at the clock on my bedside table and saw it was 8 am.

Perfect.

By the time I woke up again, it would be late afternoon. The club I liked opened at 7 pm, which would give me plenty of time to eat, shower, dress, and call a driver. I reached beside the clock and grabbed the whiskey bottle and glass I'd set out the night before. Uncapping the whiskey lid, I poured a generous glassful, then sculled it down. After returning the bottle and glass to my bedside table, I settled back in for another round of dreamless oblivion.

Chapter Five

Emerson

I FORCED my eyes awake as the sound of my phone alarm split through my head. I needed to switch it off, but could not get my brain to cooperate. Sil's voice merged with my inner psychologist's voice in condemning me. *That's what happens when you try to cope by numbing yourself with alcohol and sleeping pills and a night of dancing.* I groaned at the thought, then struggled to sit up. All right, so I used a coping mechanism, but it was only once a year. It *was not* a problem, certainly not in the 'negative coping mechanism' category, and I *was not* numb. I felt things. Too much. That was why I used 'the ritual' to get through the hardest day of my life. I had mitigated the chance of a flashback, panic attack, and other intrusive episodes. Hence, once again, the ritual had been successful.

Is that so?

Ugh. The inner objections had grown louder over the past two years. Refusing to get into an argument with my brain, I grabbed my phone from the bedside table and switched off the alarm. I had a new client coming and needed to prepare. At least I'd lucked out of a one-night stand last night, so I didn't have a woman I needed to wake and kick out while trying not to come across as a jerk. Replacing the phone, I reached for the robe at the end of my bed. An ache shot through my head, making me wince. I needed a cold shower and coffee to snap my brain back into work mode and halt any hangover that wanted to come.

Too late.

With a frown at my inner self, I stood and stumbled towards the ensuite bathroom. Before I could step inside, my phone startled me by ringing. Cursing under my breath, I turned towards the bedside table and eyed the phone's screen. Jack's name flickered across the screen. Could be important news. He'd been working on several deals for me, including radio, television, and international media. What if it was about a book deal? A sharp ache split through my head. *Nope.* I couldn't deal with a business discussion before I'd had coffee or a shower. Preferably both. I'd have to call him back. Besides, I had a new client coming. I muted the call and stepped into the bathroom.

Fifteen minutes later, I felt more awake, but the headache lingered. Getting dressed and fixing my hair became tasks as head-splitting as the rest of the morning had been. Still, I ran a comb through my hair and pull on a pair of clean, black trousers and a pale blue polo shirt without much drama. Blue apparently had a calming effect, so I wore the colour during my client meetings. Another nudge from my head told me it was well beyond coffee time. The lingering nausea in my stomach told me breakfast was a no-go. I walked to my home office––converted out of the original lounge room––at the front of my home. Inside, I stopped at the small kitchenette at the back, right corner of the office. When I opened the cupboard to retrieve a mug, I grimaced at a pain between my eyes. *Ugh*. I needed to wake up. *And sober up.* I let that comment slide while I made the coffee.

The initial sip felt like a balm to my sore head. After a few more sips, and feeling more alive, I took the mug with me to my desk, which I'd set against the back wall and beside the kitchenette. On top of my desk was the file I'd made for the new client. I sat, reviewing her details, when a light tap echoed from my home's front door. That had to be her. I closed the file and stood upright. Too fast.

'Ow.'

A fresh ache hit me in the middle of the head. Looked like the coffee hadn't helped as much as I'd thought. Drawing in a breath, I forced myself to focus. Today was not about me and my past, it was about someone else's.

I gave myself a pep talk, 'You can do this,' then walked to the office door and stopped. When I stooped to grab the black loafers I kept next to the door, I could only find one. Slipping it onto my right foot, I did a quick search for the other. It was nowhere inside my office. I stepped over the threshold and spotted the left loafer near the front door. I walked towards it, slipped on my left loafer, then reached for the doorknob.

When I opened the door, a blonde-haired woman glanced at my face, then lowered her eyes as she said, 'I have an appointment.'

I was about to introduce myself and invite her in, when something flickered familiarity within me. *Those eyes.* I'd seen them before. I'd thought how pretty they were ... it had to be *Water Woman.*

'I think I know you.'

She peered up and let her gaze assess me.

I realised I would look different to her without the cap and glasses I'd worn, so I clarified, 'From the store the other day.'

Store. I hadn't chosen that word consciously, but it was probably best not to admit I'd been heading to the Bottle-O. *And why is that, Emerson?* I pushed the thought aside, along with the accompanying twinge in my head, and refocused.

In an unsure voice, she said, 'Water Guy?'

I chuckled at the synchronicity of the similar nick-names we'd given each other. 'That's me, but most other people call me Emerson Novak. You must be Neoma?'

'Oh, yes, I am ... sorry.'

'No apology necessary. You're here for our meeting?'

Even though she'd already told me, I purposely injected a question into our small talk to get her to respond. If I could keep her talking, she would eventually feel more at ease with me, and would also learn it was safe to speak up. Using the term 'meeting' as opposed to 'ses-sion' had also been intentional. 'Meeting' had a more relaxed feel to it. Also made it sound more voluntary than the first meetings usually were. Most of my clients came through a second party. I remembered Neoma's best friend had set this up. Which meant I'd likely encounter resistance from Neoma. My social media accounts had been getting more popular of late and Jack had said the increased attention might bring more willing clients soon. Either way, I enjoyed a challenge. Always had. As evidenced from my choice to join the army to start my psychology career. My mother always said I'd never done things the easy way. On the odd occasion, she even said it with pride in her voice.

Neoma's simple answer brought me back to the present, 'Yes.'

'Come on in.'

I smiled, then took a slow step to the side to give her plenty of room to enter through the front door without bumping into me. Some trauma survivors didn't like to be touched by strangers. Especially male strangers. She took a tentative step inside, then stopped opposite me in the entry hall.

'The therapy room is to your left.' I indicated to the door I'd purposely left open to provide a subconscious atmosphere of freedom and openness. I'd also chosen to convert the lounge room into a home office because of its proximity to the front door. Clients seemed comforted by the fact there was an easy, direct escape route. 'Take a seat wherever you like.'

She nodded, then stepped into the room. I noticed the way she entered, almost sideways. Keeping her eyes on me and her internal guard up. I stayed put, lowered my gaze, and slightly exposed my neck--subtle submission signals--to put her mind at ease and show I was no threat. Once she was inside the office, I was careful to close the front door without a sudden jolt or loud bang. Tiny actions like that could trigger someone into an unwanted trauma response. I was extra careful until I learned the specific triggers for each client. With that in mind, I avoided loud footsteps as I entered after her. The office's carpet helped dull any hard footsteps my loafers would have made on hard flooring. I saw Neoma seated in the armchair closest to the door. *For a quick escape?* It would also allow her to maintain an upright and alert posture. She didn't fully trust me. Which was fine, and natural, for now. The chair choice also showed she could make decisions to protect herself. People-pleasing tendencies were not ingrained then. She glanced at the office door, indicating she might be worried about it being closed. *Closed doors with strangers. That's a possible trigger.* Noting that in my mind, I left the door open and walked towards her using slow movements. Even with the precautions, I saw it wasn't enough.

CHAPTER SIX

Neoma

THE FLASH OF A MEMORY INVADED. I couldn't stop the yelp of alarm that came out. Some part of my brain registered the person closing in on me was Emerson. *It's not them.* But the information didn't process in my body. A suffocating tightness wrapped around me. I couldn't move, I couldn't breathe, I couldn't speak. Instead, *their* sneering faces appeared opposite mine. Reality merged with my nightmares. I couldn't focus. Where was I? What was happening? Through the growing fog of my vision, I thought I saw Emerson stop in front of my chair with his hands up, like he was handing himself over to the police.

His voice sounded soft and soothing when he said, 'You're safe, Neoma. I know you're confused, but try to focus on my voice.'

The words processed as my breathing tightened

further and faces of the past intruded further into my present.

Emerson continued, 'I know your brain is saying you're somewhere else, but you're with me in my meeting room, and you're safe. I'm going to help you, but I need you to look into my eyes first.'

I must have obeyed because I was staring into a set of brown eyes that did not belong to the past. These eyes looked warm, bright, and concerned, not cruel, dark, and taunting.

'You're doing great. Now, say my name.' His gaze locked onto mine, refusing to let me look away.

The tightness in my chest loosened and the phantom images shifted back to the past. I heard my croaky voice answer as if detached from my body, 'Emerson.'

'That's right. What's my last name?'

Emerson's last name … I knew this. Cara had told me, hadn't she? Or, had Emerson told me himself? I couldn't recall with certainty.

'Neoma, I need you to focus only on my last name. What is it?'

I concentrated and soon heard myself say, 'Novak?'

'That's right.' He smiled at me. I realised the smile looked clear. The fogginess was lifting from my mind. 'Can you look around the room now and tell me three things you can see?'

What? Why?

He must have guessed what I was thinking because he explained, 'This is a grounding exercise. It's using a different part of your brain to help you switch from the past to the present, and away from emotion to logic. Nod if you think you can name three things for me?'

I nodded.

'Whenever you're ready.' He took a step back, then turned on a slight angle from me. I felt my focus shift with him, as if he were leading me where to look.

My voice sounded more controlled when I said, 'Bookcase. Plant. Rug.'

'Yes. You're doing great. What are three things you can hear?'

'Air conditioning. Birds chirping outside. My breathing.'

'Great. Now, I want you to walk around this room and touch three things. Name them as you touch them. It's the last exercise I'll get you to do. I want to make sure you're fully grounded in the present before we move on. Is that okay with you?'

I nodded then rose from the chair and took a slow walk around the room.

Stopping at the bookcase, I touched a paperback. 'Book.'

After a closer look at the book, I saw it was a romance novel. My favourite genre. Did Emerson read romance novels? An image of him browsing the aisles of the romance section in libraries and bookshops filled my mind. I almost felt like smiling at the idea. That was enough to make me refocus. Several self-help books now stood out, different from the ones the other counsellors recommended. Some sounded interesting based on their titles. One self-help book––suggested by Cara––that I'd read and found insightful was wedged between two others.

Emerson pulled me from the ponderings by saying, 'Two more.'

Walking on, I stopped at his desk and touched the first item I spotted on it, 'Silver pen.' It felt cold under my fingertips, but looked beautiful and shiny from a distance. *Much like some of the men I've dated …*

'Well done. Last one.'

I walked over to what looked like a second sitting area. A variety of seating choices––bean bags, armchairs, an old-fashioned floral chaise, stools––had been arranged around a blue-cushioned bay window. I felt a pinch of reminiscence in my heart as I touched the window frame. My late maternal grandmother used to have one like this in her house. 'Bay window.'

'Can you tell me where you are right now?'

'Standing in this room with you.'

'Fantastic job, Neoma. You should feel proud of yourself.'

Proud. Why? I realised then what he had guided me to do. Never had I come through a flashback or panic attack that fast––thanks to the book Cara had given me, I knew what these *really* were as opposed to what I had seen on TV and in movies. While I didn't feel completely back to myself, I was somewhat mentally and emotionally stable.

Astounded, I turned from the bay window to face him and somehow managed to say, 'Thank you.'

'You're welcome. By the way, that's a technique you can use whenever you feel overwhelmed. You name three things you can see and hear, then walk around as you touch three things. If you don't think you can walk, any movement helps, even if it's just clapping your hands. It can disperse agitated energy from your nervous system. It's also good if you can get your logical brain online. Try to remember the full name of somebody you don't know well or list some facts.'

Now I knew why he'd gotten me to do all of that.

'Speaking of facts, I'd like to teach you another quick technique you can use. Will that be all right with you?'

'Depends on what it is.'

He flashed a quick smile, then looked away again as he asked, 'Have you heard of a body scan?'

'Yes. I used to do …' I hesitated on saying 'I used to do them all the time'. He didn't need to know that information. Why was I telling him? I continued, 'It's when you mentally scan your body for tight spots.'

'Perfect. The Vital Signs Scan I recommend for my clients is similar. Do you think you could try it?' He looked in my direction but avoided my direct gaze.

'Yes.'

'Would you like to sit and get comfortable?'

I returned to my former chair.

Once I sat, he asked, 'Can you tell me how your heart rate is?'

I went to touch the pulse point at my wrist, but Emerson stopped me by saying, 'It's better if you *feel* it within yourself. I know it sounds kind of kooky, but the point of the Vital Signs Scan is to become aware of your body. Accuracy and so-called reality are irrelevant. It's the grounding and calming effect on the nervous system that we're after with this exercise. Focus on your heart. How is the beat rate?'

I narrowed my attention on the beat of my heart. No heavy thumps, no rapid thrums. 'It feels fine.'

'Your body temperature?'

I lifted my hand to my forehead out of habit.

Once again, Emerson cut in before I could touch my forehead, saying, 'Feel it with your awareness, not your hand. Do you understand what I mean?'

As Emerson had said, the idea might have sounded kooky to some, but from years of meditating, I knew what he meant. I nodded, lowered my hand, then focused on how my body temperature felt. No goosebumps, which meant I wasn't too cold despite the air-conditioning. No sweat, so I wasn't too hot. 'Also fine.'

'How's your breath rate?'

I concentrated on my breathing. No sharp intakes of air or breath-holding going on. The rate had normalised. Probably because I was focusing on it now. I knew from a book I'd edited at my work that breathing was one of a handful of bodily functions that humans could consciously control, and thinking about one's breathing rate usually meant it changed. Had that been Emerson's goal? His former words replayed … *become aware of your body … it's the grounding and calming effect.* Had getting me to focus on the physiological factors that can appear when someone is feeling anxious or overwhelmed––like a rapid heart and breath rate, or a heated body––helped to calm me by making me take conscious control of my nervous system?

Clever.

'Neoma, how's your breathing?'

My overanalysing had taken longer than I'd thought, based on Emerson's repetition of the question. 'It's okay now.'

'Great. That's all the Vital Signs Scan involves. Check your heart rate, body temperature, and breathing. It's another way to get your logical brain online. Whenever you get triggered, the emotional centres of your brain have been agitated. You want to switch back to your logical centres as soon as possible.'

'Okay.'

He walked towards his desk, turned, and leaned against it with his hands on either side of him, holding onto the desk. Looking relaxed, he said, 'The Vital Signs Scan can help you calm down because it's a sneaky way of hijacking your brain and nervous system. If you're focusing on your breathing especially, and want it to regulate, it regulates.'

'Ha! I knew it.'

Emerson jumped, clearly startled by my outburst. I brought my hands to my mouth.

Through my fingers, I stammered, 'Sorry, I--'

'No apology necessary.'

He brought his gaze to mine. I spied the same warmth in his eyes that I'd spotted during the flashback moments ago. Why did it make me feel calm when he looked at me like that? Who needed 'scans' and fancy 'exercises' when they had *those eyes* to focus on? The insanity of that thought struck me. Emerson wasn't some hypnotist with magic eyes ... at least, I didn't think so. Who knew? Maybe hypnotism was another of his unorthodox therapies. I blinked to break from his gaze, and my whirring thoughts, then lowered my hands from my mouth to my lap.

'Are you all right?'

'Yes.'

'You stopped yourself from speaking just now. That's called "self-censoring". Is there anything you'd like to say that you didn't get to say?'

I shook my head ... and caught the irony of not having spoken my answer. Another instance of self-censoring?

He didn't comment on it, saying instead, 'For future reference, feel free to say anything you want with me. I'm not easily upset or offended, all right?'

'Okay.'

That's what I said, even though I wanted to snort in derision. Everyone said they wouldn't get offended if you were honest, then proceeded to get enraged when you *were* honest. Like the line from that famous movie said, most people couldn't handle the truth.

He gave me an assessing look. It felt like he could see through me, which sent a subtle, pleasant tingly feeling through me, as well as a thick, icky feeling of shame. What if he saw too much?

Relief filled me up when he said, 'The next time you get triggered, try the "three things exercise" or the "Vital Signs Scan" and see what happens. You can use them together as well. Or a combination of the other exercises I'll be showing you during our meetings. Use whatever works for you.'

I nodded, then remembered to speak, 'Okay.'

He glanced at me, avoiding my eyes. The other counsellors had almost forced direct eye contact on me. It had felt invasive. Emerson made eye contact at times, but it felt natural. Not forced or intrusive. If anything, it was comforting and reassuring when he did it.

His next words brought me from my thoughts, 'Keep in mind that nothing is one hundred percent effective, one hundred percent of the time, for one hundred percent of people. Though these techniques might not work all the time, they do work *some* of the time, which makes them beneficial to have in your toolbox.'

'Okay.'

Unsure of what to do next, I waited for him to continue.

Chapter Seven

Emerson

Once I'd realised Neoma was having a flashback, I'd stared into her eyes, the same way I did whenever my clients needed something solid to focus on, and ... when the look in her jade-green eyes had morphed from fear to trust, a knowing warmth had enveloped me. That reaction, from her as well as myself, confirmed I was on the right track. I felt positive about our meeting so far. Except for one factor: Neoma baffled me. She'd hinted at having a forthright personality, yet other times she seemed shut down. I knew this was trauma related, but still, who was the real Neoma Alban? In the silence, I took a moment to assess her. Even though her body language and clothes screamed 'ignore me,' there was something more I caught in her seated posture. The way she held her shoulders back showed a steady confidence that had been there once. Before whatever trauma had come her way.

What had happened to her? Whenever a second party contacted me, I insisted on not knowing the details of the trauma. That was up to my client to divulge, if and when, they chose. Trauma survivors often had difficulty with trust. I'd learned that starting off with all their personal information without their explicit consent was not the best way to earn their trust. Which I needed to keep earning. Despite seeing the hint of confidence in Neoma, the overwhelming message I received from her was not knowing the 'right' thing to do. Had she developed 'people-pleasing' tendencies I hadn't clocked yet? Some trauma survivors used that as a subconscious defence mechanism, a way their psyche kept them safe. Our subsequent meetings would clarify whether people-pleasing was a problem and if it was something she had always done, or the result of whatever trauma she had survived.

Neoma's behaviour thus far enabled me to discern pieces of her possible trauma history. Her dark blue denim jeans and navy jumper were too baggy for her petite frame, and too heavy for a mild spring day, suggesting she didn't want attention drawn to her body. As did her blonde hair, pulled into a rough bun. A thick fringe covered her eyebrows to the point of almost being in her eyes. That type of fringe in trauma survivors could be a subconscious hiding tactic, another defence mechanism. Confirming my theory that she didn't want attention. These could also be signs exhibiting the continuation of a post-trauma 'fade' response: behaviours which help her 'fade into the background.' I glanced at Neoma's face and sensed a growing discomfort coming from her. I realised then that Neoma had her hands on her lap in front of her, with her gaze directed at the floor. She was waiting for me to continue. The meeting needed to get moving again. My observations could wait until she'd left, and I made notes in her file.

Drawing in a breath, I said, 'You must be exhausted.' Flashbacks and panic attacks could be terrifying, disorienting, and tiring.

She hesitated, glanced up, back down, then said, 'I'm okay.'

Not the complete truth. Even with the movement element I'd incorporated into the 'three things' technique––to help discharge residual nervous energy from her body––her eyes had betrayed her still somewhat shaken state. Which was normal after the trauma response I'd just witnessed. I needed to help her relax.

'Did you want something to drink?'

Her gaze whipped up, and a startled look passed over her face before she said, 'It's a little early for that, isn't it?' Before I could explain I'd meant something non-alcoholic, she looked down and half-whispered, 'I don't drink anymore.'

I don't drink *anymore.* Intriguing word choice. Alcohol could be a possible trigger for her. Had it been a coping mechanism? Problematic drug and alcohol use was high in trauma survivors. Had I stumbled across a sore point? That made two possible triggers: *doors* and *alcohol.* I would need to make a note in her file.

'I didn't mean alcohol. I was thinking more like juice, soft drink … or bottled water.'

She glanced up at my pause and subsequent emphasis on the water. I'd done it hoping to lighten the mood and strengthen our therapeutic connection based on a shared experience. Instead, she fidgeted with her fingers. Definite sore point.

'I'm fine, thank you.'

'Would you like me to open the window?' I pointed at the bay window to clarify.

She shrugged. 'Whatever's easier for you.'

My questions had appeared innocuous, but they were diagnostic tools, which enabled me to see where clients were when it came to voicing their preferences and asserting their personal power. So far, Neoma had shown she could assert personal power––via her choice in seat––as well as her preferences––saying no to a drink. Minor examples, but a positive start. If she could assert herself on the small things, she could for the more important things, even if she didn't right now. Her latest response to the window was more ambiguous. It could be a people-pleasing answer––she didn't want to be any 'trouble'––or she didn't care. Either way, I would write the observations in my notes after the meeting. My next step involved explaining to Neoma how the meeting would progress. I kept my body language open and remained leaning against my desk.

'In a moment, I am going to divide the room. This will be your area for all our meetings and will include unobstructed access to the door. I will not invade your area unless there is an emergency, or you request it, so you can move around as much as you want. You can also rearrange furniture and bring in items that bring you comfort. I will not stop you if you choose to leave at any time. Is all of that all right with you?'

'I guess so.'

Another wishy-washy answer. We could do voice work if I kept noticing she needed to become more confident and definite in her answers.

'Most people are curious about my methods. I'm not sure what Cara has told you, but you won't need to talk about anything you don't want to talk about. Our meetings will mostly involve breathing, voice, scanning, and movement exercises. These exercises are supplemented with reading and writing exercises between our sessions.' She raised an eyebrow at this admission. Most of my clients did. Hell, my former colleagues had done the same when I'd explained my new direction. It didn't bother me. I knew my methods were based on solid research. Other than that, the people I had helped were all the evidence I needed. 'I'll also follow up with a casual phone call between our formal meetings to check in and give you a chance to ask questions. Speaking of, any questions so far?'

She shook her head.

Hmm. She doesn't talk much. Her answers had been mostly two or three words. And, she self-censored whenever she *was* about to say more than a few words. I thought back to my explanation of the Vital Signs Scan. It had seemed like she'd been about to tell me she'd performed plenty of body scans, but she had paused and glossed over her words, so I couldn't be one hundred percent certain. *She doesn't give away information.* Why? Was it something she did with everyone or just strangers? Men in general? Was it trauma related? Or her natural personality?

Based on what I'd seen so far, I understood why her best friend had referred Neoma to me. Neoma displayed multiple signs of what I called 'post-traumatic stress reactions.' I didn't like using the more popular term 'post-traumatic stress disorder.' Neoma's reactions shouldn't be classified as a 'disorder,' when they were the brain's normal response to trauma. Several well-respected authorities on the subject agreed with me. Under-talking could be a post-traumatic stress reaction. Something else I needed to note in her file later.

Even though I didn't require a history, and I rarely asked, most clients ended up sharing snippets of their experiences with me. Neoma might be different. I might never know what happened to her. For some inexplicable reason, that possibility niggled at my stomach. The sensation startled me. I hadn't *wanted* to know a client's story in years. Why was Neoma different? Maybe because she seemed such a closed book that she piqued my curiosity?

With that thought, I said, 'How about we get started?'

I could have said, 'Let's get started.' However, I tried to turn as many statements into questions as possible, to give my clients both the appearance of choice and the option to disagree.

After Neoma nodded, I walked to the bay window and pulled out the concertina-style room divider set into the side of it. The divider screen was decorated with pink cherry blossoms. When extended, the divider separated the sitting area from my office part of the room. This system I'd devised provided my client with a deeper sense of safety because it did not disrupt a clear path to the door and ensured I couldn't easily invade their personal space. A wonderful lesson in boundaries for clients who regularly had none.

Through the divider, I said, 'Give me a moment to set up, then we can start.'

'Okay.' She didn't sound confident or enthusiastic.

I hope that changes.

An excited swell in my chest made me linger on the thought. It seemed Neoma had stirred up my original excitement for psychology. An excitement I assumed had died eight years ago, when it had become overshadowed by my own experiences. Psychology had devolved into a job I was good at. Or so I'd thought. Was my enthusiasm finally coming back after all these years? If so, how would it affect my practice? Would it push me to become a better trauma recovery facilitator? As the possibility settled in my chest, I continued preparing for the official start of our meeting.

CHAPTER EIGHT

Neoma

WAS it strange he was behind a screen? It felt like he was using it to avoid me. Why? Did he do this with every client? The screen was set into the wall, like a pull-out curtain, so he must. *He admitted his methods are unconventional.* Cara had told me that as well. I shrugged and looked around my 'area,' as Emerson had referred to it. *Emerson.* Not a common name … *yeah, because Neoma is.* I released a soft snort at the thought. Unusual names were not as fun as some people assumed. I'd spent most of my life spelling my name to strangers. He'd probably experienced the same thing.

He interrupted my thoughts, saying, 'Are you ready?'

No.

'Yes.'

'Great. As a reminder, my therapy focuses on breathing, body and movement, voice work, romance reading, and writing exercises.'

One part of that spiel stood out. '*Romance books* will be part of my therapy?'

'They might.'

'Okay …' They were my favourite books, but how were they *therapy*?

I sensed him grin, as if he knew something I didn't, then he added, 'You aren't at that stage yet. Before we begin––' *We haven't begun yet?* What the heck? '––I'll tell you a bit more about me.'

I refocused long enough to blurt out, 'Okay.'

'I have a master's degree in psychology and have worked extensively with trauma clients. Though I was a practising psychologist early in my career, I became a trauma recovery facilitator so I could branch out into unorthodox healing modalities.'

'Okay.' *No mention of the army. Should I ask?* No. *Keep your loud mouth shut. That's what got you into trouble last time.*

I swallowed down the thoughts that wanted to come with the warning and was grateful when he continued, shutting down my brain, 'During our meetings togeth-er––' *Meetings, plural.* That was a touch presumptuous of him. There would not be anymore. But he didn't need to know that yet. All I had to do was play along to make Cara happy. I'd agreed to attend for Cara. If this was what she wanted, it was the least I could do. I zoned back into his words, 'We will focus on one of the exercises I mentioned before. Then, I'll assign a related reading, writ-ing, or other exercise to carry out between our meetings.'

Wait, 'other exercise'? What did that mean? Should I be worried? He continued before the concern could take proper hold in my brain, 'We can discuss the results of the exercises at our next meeting. Of course, you do not have to do the exercises, nor must you discuss anything with me you don't want to discuss. Does that suit you?'

It felt like he'd added that last part for my benefit; as if he somehow sensed that I was not into this. Or, had Cara warned him I might be resistant?

'Okay.' It wasn't an overt agreement, but could be perceived that way. Once again proving to Cara that I'd tried. *Or proving that trying isn't even an option?* I ignored the unspoken comment as Emerson talked again.

'If you look at the coffee table in the middle of the sitting area, you will see some items on it.'

I glanced at the glass, oval table and saw a pink floral book with the word 'journal' written in gold lettering at the top. A slim, metallic, rose-gold coloured pen sat on top of it.

'Can you see them?'

'Yes.'

'They are yours to use throughout our time together. Your meeting fees cover the cost, so don't worry about that.'

'Oh, I …' Was at a loss as to what to say. My recently acquired instinct to mistrust anything a man gave me for free swooped in. Did I take them or not? *It's part of the costs.* This wasn't a gift to butter me up or give me a false sense of security. Emerson had given it with no expectations or assumptions. There *were* some men who did thoughtful things just because they wanted to. Besides, this was part of the therapy fees. I cleared my throat and said, 'Thanks. They're pretty.'

'I'm glad you like them. There's something about the pen-to-paper connection that loosens the brain up. Any questions before we dive in?'

Hadn't he already asked that?

I shook my head. 'No … actually, yes. Do I really not have to talk about … things?'

'That's correct.'

'Do I have to talk at all?'

'Only if you want to.'

Yes! This was going to be a breeze. 'I don't want to.'

'That's fine. I'm comfortable with silence.'

I frowned. His relaxed manner renewed the developed suspicion within me. No counsellor I'd been to so far had been this easy-going.

'This sounds … too simple.'

I thought I heard him chuckle before he said, 'Tell me that *after* I've given you your first task.'

That made me curious. 'What's the first task?'

'Breathe.'

CHAPTER NINE

BREATHING. *That's what I did for most of the alleged 'therapy session' Cara booked for me today. Can you believe that? Breathing! Okay, meditation I get. Breathing while meditating, yep. Totally get it. Even breathing while remaining mindful, which is basically what he taught me, is fine. But ... how is that supposed to be 'therapy?' Even if I think of it as 'unorthodox therapy,' it feels like I'm missing something. To say it was different to my experience with the other counsellors is an understatement. Ack. Am I wasting my time? Body scans and breathing. That had been the basic sum total of our session.*

Okay, he called them 'Vital Sign Scans' (which are quite clever when I think about it) and 'mindful slow breathing,' but it seemed more like a new age, spiritual, hippie class than a therapy session! What was he going to get me to do next: meditate on one leg while humming the tune of a kirtan song and lighting incense? Ah! At least he didn't ask me to try the stereo-

typical way of meditating ('remove all thoughts from your mind'). The last few times I've tried to do that hasn't helped. That technique has brought memories back instead. Anyway, you can see, Diary, why I'm hesitant and haven't decided if I'm going to go ahead with our next session, even though he's booked me in for about three weeks from now. He said it was my choice.

In the meantime, he asked me to practice the vital sign scans and mindful slow breathing at least ten times between now and then. I'm supposed to use this journal to write down my experiences. Speaking of this journal, Emerson gave it to me. This pen I'm writing with, too. I'd felt unsure and suspicious at first (why was he giving me something and what did he want in return?) but he'd said it was included in the fees. I didn't get any weird vibe about that, so I feel okay about having them now. They're pretty, too.

Now that I'm writing about the session (he calls them 'meetings'), I can see that whenever I got triggered, Emerson would drop his voice, so it had this low, soft edge to it. Very soothing. Did he do that on purpose? I like it when he does that. He helped me through a flashback-panic attack with that voice. But, there were some odd things about his methods, like, he insisted on sitting behind a screen! But, he seemed calm and easy-going. Emerson said I can use this journal for other things as well, not just the therapy exercises he sets. Not sure if I will? Anyway, back to the exercises. I'm not sure what to write about the 'mindful slow breathing' he took me through, because nothing much happened. I found it hard to concentrate on the breathing, which I know is normal from my own previous meditation practice, and I am rusty. He also confirmed it was normal. My stupid 'monkey mind' kept swinging everywhere as well. I *couldn't focus on the breathing or settle my thoughts. I know I'll get better, he said that too, but it's frustrating being someone who has meditated for many years and is finding it difficult. When I'd been doing the breathing and he'd noticed I was getting upset, he'd said to 'notice without judgement.' I know that! I also know he wasn't trying to be patronising (he couldn't know that I used to meditate when I hadn't told him), but it's easier said than done. He hasn't been inside my head lately.*

Anyway, when it came to the breathing, Emerson had said, 'Breath is life. As long as you are breathing, you know you are alive.' Or some such thing like that. He'd shown me a new breathing technique nobody else has ever shown me, too. You inhale slowly to the count of four. Then, hold your breath for a count of two, breathe out slowly to a count of five, and finish by holding your breath for another count of two. Emerson had said, 'Anytime you breathe in, you want to breathe out at a slower rate. It's been proven to calm your nervous system.' He'd said the emphasis should be on slow *breathing as opposed to* deep *breathing. He said some people get confused by the command to 'breathe deep,' and tend to take a quick and big breath in from the upper chest rather than a slow, controlled breath from the diaphragm/stomach. Diaphragmatic and belly breathing is something I've done before, so it wasn't much of a stretch for me. I'm supposed to set a timer for five minutes and do the breathing until the timer goes off. I've got to remember to 'notice, not judge' any thoughts and feelings that come up as well. And, breathe from my belly. Then, I'm supposed to write about what happened in this journal.*

There was also this technique he showed me in the office, when I got triggered. It's naming three things I can see, hear, and touch, then trying to recall a fact. Apparently, it uses a different part of your brain and can help you calm the trigger. It worked in the session, so I've written it down here in case I need to remember and use it another time.

The 'vital signs scan' I talked about before includes focusing on my heart and breath rates and body temperature after an episode to get the body and nervous system to calm.

Emerson said I can repeat the 'name three things' exercise or the 'vital signs scan' or focus on 'mindful slow breathing' if I'm triggered. He called them 'techniques for my toolbox.' Even though it sounds a little hippy dippy, I don't mind. Geez, I've just realised how much I've scribbled. Most of it is nonsense, but oddly, I feel pretty good after dribbling on. Maybe there is something to this journaling thing? Maybe even this 'unorthodox counselling' thing? At the very least, I've gotten a pretty journal and pen out of it.

I glanced at the pen in my hand and the journal sitting on my outstretched legs. I'd arrived back at Cara's house a short time ago and had gone straight to my bedroom, where I'd hopped onto the bed to have my usual afternoon nap. Except, that's not what I'd done. Somehow, I'd ended up writing in the journal. I couldn't even recall when I'd made that decision.

I shrugged and returned my attention back to the session. Aside from the flashback, it had been easy, much easier than I'd anticipated. Emerson had done most of the talking. I'd felt relatively relaxed about it, which was new. The other counsellors I'd seen had left me feeling high anxiety levels. Even now, that sense of calmness lingered. *Interesting.* Was it the breathing exercises, journaling, or not having to talk that had created the feeling? Maybe it had been all of them? Was there a chance this therapy thing could work?

The sound of the front door opening made me narrow my attention. Probably Cara, but that didn't stop my heart from reacting. It felt like it was trying to keep in time with an ultra-fast polka dance. What if it was someone else? What if it was *them*? What if––

Breathe.

The unspoken command came before I was conscious of thinking it, cutting off the incessant 'what ifs.' Closing my eyes, I focused on the breathing rhythm Emerson had taught me.

Four. Two. Five. Two.

Four. Two. Five. Two.

Four. Two. Five. Two––

'Neo? It's me. I'm coming to your room.'

I exhaled a long, slow, relieved breath. It *was* only Cara. 'Okay.'

A moment later, my best friend opened the bedroom door and peeked around it. 'How'd it go?'

Her expression was hopeful, but not expectant. She had come to accept that I probably wouldn't go back.

I hesitated, not wanting to get her hopes up too much, because I wasn't certain where I stood on the matter either, then answered, 'I knew him.'

Cara raised an eyebrow in obvious interest. 'What? How did you know him?'

'Remember when I bought the water at the shops for you the other day?'

'Yeah.'

'He's the guy who helped me when I dropped them.'

Her eyes widened as she took a step into the room. 'Emerson Novak is *Water Guy?*'

I'd told her the basics of the story, including my nickname for him. 'Yep.'

'Did he remember you?'

'He did.'

'Was it awkward?'

'Nope.' Which, now I was thinking about it, had been a blessing. The fact we'd technically met beforehand had probably added to my settling in with him faster. That, and him helping me through a flashback.

'That's good. How was the session?'

'It was … interesting.'

'Does that mean you'll go back?' The look on her face edged closer to hopeful.

'Maybe.'

Cara grinned before she said, 'I'm taking that as a "yes." I'm so proud of you.' She went to swoop in for a hug––the way we had in the past whenever one of us was excited–– but I saw when she remembered I could get jumpy from being touched these days. A recognisable flicker of disappointment appeared in her eyes before understanding replaced it. She stepped away and said, 'I'm going to make you a special dinner to celebrate. Don't argue. It's time you ate something more exciting than you usually have.'

She didn't wait for an answer before leaving.

'Looks like we're celebrating.' My stomach added a grumble at the prospect of something beyond the microwave nuggets and instant mash I'd been surviving on. I held a hand to my stomach to settle its anticipatory noises, then whispered, 'Traitor.'

Chapter Ten

Emerson

Sitting at my office desk after our session, I jotted as much information as I could while the meeting was still fresh in my mind. Yes, I preferred handwritten notes rather than typed ones. The mind-pen connection accessed a part of me that the typical computer typing didn't. I recommended this technique to all my clients.

As had happened several times since Neoma left, my mind throbbed. It had been idiotic to schedule a meeting the day after the anniversary, when I'd known I'd be drinking. *Lesson learned.* I read over some of the notes I'd taken so far: 'Neoma's reactions and behaviour, and gut feeling, are telling me she is hyperaroused (e.g. the flash-back she had, awareness of the door, alert to mention of alcohol). Therefore, her trauma is likely to have involved a prolonged major incident or multiple incidents.'

Once-off trauma survivors commonly exhibited hypoaroused responses--slower, numbing reactions versus the more agitated, panicky reactions of hyper-arousal. Of course, there were exceptions. Trauma effects were not a 'one-size-fits-all' checklist. But, for now, I was leading towards a more chronic or prolonged trauma experience for Neoma.

I continued reading my notes: 'Whatever her personal pronouns or sexual orientation, she presents as a female.'

That information was significant, because, being female, her trauma most likely involved an element of physical, verbal, or sexual assault. Or all three.

In my notes, I'd also commented on that. 'The hyper-arousal reactions, wanting to hide her body, and presenting as female lead me to believe her trauma involves a sexual element. The perpetrator would statisti-cally be male. As such, her level of distrust towards me could be high.'

I would need to tread lightly in our future meetings to make her feel comfortable and safe. My professional conduct would need to remain high to minimise unequal power dynamics, create an atmosphere of free communi-cation, and develop trust between us. I paused. All of that would only be possible if she came back. Would Neoma keep the appointment we'd arranged in three weeks? I wasn't sure. So far, all my clients had come back for a second meeting. And a third and fourth. Some had stopped after four sessions--because they'd learned enough to move on without me--but none had ever left after the first. The high retention rate, in my opinion, was because I took the process slowly, and built up the clients' resilience as well as their trust in me, and themselves. The fact they didn't have to talk about uncomfortable topics also seemed to guarantee return visits.

When I'd confirmed with Neoma that she wouldn't have to talk, the information had obviously relaxed her. Was that enough to guarantee her return? I wasn't sure. *You haven't lost a client before the fourth session before ...* Even though my brain tried to convince me, a stab of doubt lingered. What would happen to her if she didn't return? Anyone with eyes could see she was standing on the edge––an ambiguous spot which could result in her slipping into the abyss or taking steps back to safety. Which option would she choose?

An unexpected energy surged through me at the question––further confirmation of the excitement she had renewed for my career. I couldn't let Neoma fall into the darkness. I knew what that was like. It was easier, though not easy, to catch yourself while you were standing on the edge than it was to claw your way up from the bottom. I couldn't let her take another step towards the edge. But how could I prevent it when she was resistant?

After a moment, an idea hit. *Reconnection with life.* I uncovered the activities a client enjoyed and worked that into the treatment plan, therefore make it more compelling. Reconnection with life was an important process in trauma recovery. There had to be something Neoma was passionate about. Trauma survivors often lost the desire for their usual interests. Even so, she likely dropped hints. What had I detected about her in the meeting that could be a clue to her interests? She had given more than a cursory glance at the books on my shelves, which hinted at a love for reading. There had also been a popular sports team's logo on the front of her jumper in the session. Though lots of non-sporty people followed sports teams, I still sensed that she had been physically active, or even belonged to some sort of team herself.

I could bring in book therapy easily enough, as it was already part of my program. Of course, I would need to wait for the right moment. I could also task her with attending an event, sporting or otherwise. Again, at the right time. This was still a solid starting point. That realisation made me smile. My brain hadn't worked like that, so inspired to find a solution, for years. *Since* it *had happened.* I swallowed that thought away and instead focused on the positives that had come from the brainstorming. Working with Neoma had refuelled the enthusiasm for psychology that had been lying dormant inside of me. She had been the kindling I'd needed to spark a dwindling flame. I would do whatever it took to fan that flame and, in the process, help her. No matter what I had to do, she *would* be coming to see me for a second session.

How could I do that?

I went to jot down ideas for getting her to return, but my phone rang. I half-expected to see Neoma's name on the screen when I grabbed my phone from its place on my desk. Instead, it was Jack. I hadn't returned his call. This time, I answered.

'Hello, Trauma Guru.'

I groaned. 'You know I hate that nickname.'

'I do, but a catchy nickname helps with brand recognition, remember?'

'I remember.'

My mind kept flicking back to Neoma as Jack carried on the conversation. Though I only caught the occasional word or phrase––'the contract', 'nearly there', 'international'––by the time we hung up, I had a plan for getting Neoma back to see me. And no idea what Jack had called me about.

CHAPTER ELEVEN

Neoma

An unknown number showed up on my phone's screen. I usually ignored unknown numbers, so I'm not sure why I answered, but I did.

The sound of the voice on the other end made me jump from shock when he said, 'Hello, Neoma. It's Emerson Novak.'

'Hi.' My voice sounded shaky. *Ah*. Why was he calling?

'Is now a good time to talk?'

I glanced around my bedroom. Even though it was midday, the drawn curtains made the room look darker and later than that. Dirty clothes piled up on the chair near the window. The bin under the vanity table beside the chair piled over with trash. Three empty water glasses blocked the space on my bedside table. The bed was unmade. I bolted to the curtains and yanked them open, then kicked the bottles under the bed as I pulled up the twisted blankets at the bottom of the bed. Halfway through, I stopped, realising Emerson couldn't see any of the mess. Why was I cleaning?

'Neoma?'

'Sorry, yes. We can talk.'

'This is my check in call. How have you been since our meeting?'

I sat on the end of the bed. 'Fine.'

'Have you had a chance to practise the exercises?'

'Yes.'

'Which have you found the most helpful?'

'Mm. Not sure?'

'All right, what's been the most challenging part about them?'

'I don't know?'

'I see.' He paused, then asked, 'Can you tell me how you're finding the journal writing?'

'It's okay.'

'Meaning?'

'I don't mind it.'

'Do you think you can keep it up?'

'Yes.'

'What about the other exercises?'

'Yep.'

'I meant, have you tried them?'

'Oh, okay. Yes.'

He paused a moment, then said in a non-judgemental tone, 'You don't give much away, do you?'

I lowered my head. 'Sorry, I--'

'Please stop apologising.' From someone else, those words could have sounded sharp. But from Emerson, it sounded friendly and caring. *Warm*. 'You don't need to apologise for who you are. You don't need to apologise for having an opinion. And you don't need to apologise for taking up space. Do you understand?'

I felt my throat tighten with emotion. I *did* understand. The old me had practically lived by that motto: *no apologies*. It's just that I hadn't allowed myself to be that person for months now. Not since that night.

'Neoma?'

I cleared my throat. 'I'm here.'

'I'm sorry for upsetting you.'

He apologised …

'Wait. You're allowed to apologise, but I'm not.'

I sensed him smile. 'You're allowed to apologise, but not when it's for being yourself. It's always best to save a sorry for when it's actually needed, such as when you upset someone.'

'You didn't upset me. I mean, you did, but not in a bad way.'

'I upset you in a good way?'

'Yes.'

'That's … good … I think.'

I laughed, and the sound shocked me into silence. That sort of relaxed and genuine display of happiness hadn't happened in months. Emerson laughed then. Where the sound of my own had turned me momentarily mute, his stunned me. His laughter was like a favourite song sliding into your ears and hooking into your brain. *What a lovely sound.* I realised I was smiling. Something else I hadn't done for months.

Emerson continued, 'Have you used them since our meeting?'

'Yes, and the scanning and naming exercises you taught me.'

'Really? I'm impressed.'

That fluffed my heart out a bit. 'Why?'

'It can take some time to adjust to them, and I threw a few exercises at you all at once. Well done for giving them all a shot.'

I shrugged. Tackling multiple tasks had been part of my job. I was used to it. 'Thanks.'

'You're welcome. There's something else I wanted to discuss with you. I've had a spot free up on Friday next week. Do you think you'd be able to take it?'

Friday next week.

'You want me to move our session time?'

'If you don't mind.'

'That's a week sooner than we'd planned.'

I nibbled on my bottom lip to settle the nerves that came with a question: was I ready for another session that soon? Had I even decided I would go back?

'Can you make it?'

I'm not sure if I surprised him or myself more when my voice answered, 'Sure.'

'Great. I'll book you in.' He paused a moment, then said, 'On that note, I should leave you to your day. Thank you for agreeing to the new time.'

'No problem.'

We said our goodbyes and hung up. I remained at the

edge of the bed, staring ahead in shock. Had I really agreed to an earlier session time when I hadn't even been sure I would attend at all? Emerson had brilliant persuasion skills, I'd give him that. Still, I did a body scan and discovered I didn't seem to be bothered by it. No tense body parts. In fact, part of me seemed to be eager for another session.

To myself, I muttered, 'Huh, imagine that.'

I peered around the bedroom. It bordered on pig-pen disgusting. I couldn't believe Cara hadn't pulled me up on it. *Time to clean up ...*

Chapter Twelve

Emerson

I'm going to trauma recovery facilitator hell. I'd told a small white lie about having had a 'spot free up.' But it was part of my plan. I *knew* I could help her; I just had to get her to believe that.

The sound of my phone ringing cut into my thoughts. My stomach jolted. *Please don't be Neoma changing her mind.* With hesitation, I glanced to the side of my desk where I'd placed my phone. Sil's name flashed on the screen. Relief at the sight must have zapped my judgement because the next thing I knew, I'd picked up the phone and answered.

After our initial greetings, he said, 'I've got two free tickets for the rugby league next month, if you want them for you and your dad?'

If I didn't know his methods almost as well as my own, I'd swear this was a 'reconnecting with life' ploy.

'I'll have to get back to you. Work is getting hectic.'

'All right.'

He sounded disappointed, so a stab of guilt passed through my chest. Sil had persisted in being there for me, even after I'd left the army.

He added, 'Let me know if you change your mind.'

'I will. Thanks for the call.'

'Are you trying to get rid of me?'

'Was there something else?'

'I thought we could have a proper talk.'

Ah. There it was. The *real* purpose of his call. He was asking if I wanted to take him up on his annual therapy offer since the anniversary had passed. Yes, I could see the irony, considering I'd carried out a similar ploy on Neoma.

'Sorry, Sil. It'll have to wait for another time.'

'I'll see you for our next check-in, then. You know my door is open, if you need a chat before then.'

'Thanks, Sil. I'll let you know.'

Translation: I'll call you when the fires of hell turn into icicles.

The tone of his voice told me he had caught onto the underlying message in my words, but he didn't comment on it further when he said, 'Make sure you do.'

'I will.'

Not.

We said our goodbyes, and, in the silence, I returned to my notes on Neoma. At the top of a fresh page, I wrote:

she has confirmed her attendance at the next meeting. Once the words were on paper, I allowed myself a victorious smile. I would see her again.

Chapter Thirteen

Neoma

THE SOUND of Cara opening her bedroom door made me flick off the internet search I'd been carrying out. I placed my phone face down on the kitchen counter where I sat, brought a spoonful of cereal to my mouth, and replayed the scant details I'd found out about Emerson Novak. With two days until our rescheduled second session, I'd become increasingly curious about him.

He'd left the army with an honourable discharge several years ago ... after receiving some fancy award for bravery. Granted, I was ignorant of the inner workings of the army, but why would an army psychologist receive an award for bravery? Had he saved someone's life? I hadn't been able to discover specific details. That was both frustrating and interesting. What had he done to warrant an award? And why were the details secret? Either it was classified information, or I was terrible at internet searching. I could not find general information about his time served, either. The only information available suggested he had been sent into war zones because of his expertise in war-related trauma. *Finding that kind of information probably wasn't too unusual.* How many army recruits had information about their time served up on the internet? Still, the secret award looped in my brain. That was unusual.

Cara walked from the hallway and into the kitchen, cutting off further musings. When she saw me, she stopped short, a clear look of surprise on her face. 'You're up ... and eating.'

I could understand her reaction. She had been waking me up and practically force-feeding me every morning for months. I couldn't explain it, but something had switched on inside me this past week. Almost as if Emerson's breathing exercises had, figuratively, breathed life back into my soul. That had made me curious about the person I could be from now on. I knew how nonsensical all of that would sound if I tried to verbalise it to Cara.

Instead, I smiled, then said, 'Good morning, Bestie.'

She smiled at the term of endearment. 'Good morning yourself.' I was grateful when she didn't harp on about it. Instead, she grabbed a bottle of water from the fridge and said, 'I'm heading out for a run.'

That was when I noticed she was in her running gear. The sight stirred fun memories of the two of us pounding the pavements together.

I nodded at my cereal bowl. 'Let me finish this and I'll come with you.'

She hesitated, raising an eyebrow. 'You will?'

'Yeah. It's been a while.' Before all of this had happened, Cara and I had gone out running together at least twice a week. The cardio helped with my volleyball training and her swimming. It was time to get back into it. I'd been slumping and inactive for too long.

Cara tried to hide the shock that crept into her expression, but I saw it before she replied, 'I'll wait out front. See you in ten.'

'Okay.'

I slurped the last of my cereal, then took the plate to the sink. Five minutes later, I'd slipped on socks and sneakers and grabbed a small backpack that contained my phone, keys, and wallet. At the last second, I remembered to grab a bottle of water from the fridge. Cara enjoyed running almost as much as swimming, and she would motivate me to push myself during or runs, which meant water was essential. I'd long thought my best friend would make a brilliant personal trainer, but she loved her consultant office job too much.

When I closed the fridge door, I caught sight of my hair. As had become habit, I'd finger-combed my hair that morning, then pulled it into what could only be described as an extra messy 'messy bun'. I raised my eyebrows in horror. How long had I been going out with my hair looking like that?

I ran to the bathroom, pulled out a brush, and yanked at my hair until it was easier to style into a proper messy bun. A glance at my face made me balk. Black rings under my eyes, sick-pale skin, and cracked lips made me look like I was close to meeting the Grim Reaper. In the past, I would have put on some makeup before leaving the house. Even going for a run with Cara, I would have applied tinted sunscreen at a minimum. There had been a time when I'd taken pride in caring for myself. I sighed at the memory. I didn't have the energy for a full face. But I needed to protect my skin from both my neglect and the sun. Decided, I slapped on a thin layer of sunscreen, dotted concealer over the black under-eye rings, and swiped clear lip balm over my neglected lips.

There, much better. With that thought, I saw my outfit. Though the loose fitting, marle tracksuit pants and black t-shirt I wore weren't 'on trend' by anyone's assessment, they were clean and comfortable. *No time to change.* Cara would be getting restless. I shrugged and walked out the front door. It wasn't like anyone important would be wandering through my neighbourhood, so it didn't matter what I wore. I glanced up and saw the clouds were a puffy, light-grey colour, with the sun nestled in halfway behind them. That meant the weather would be bearable for the run, especially if Cara pushed me right to my limit. *Which she has a talent for.* When I closed the front door behind me, Cara looked me up and down. The way she quirked an eyebrow told me she'd noticed my hair and face. And my outfit. I caught the way she bit her bottom lip. She wanted to say something but was stopping herself.

Rather than commenting, she said, 'Ready to go?'

God, I appreciated her. More than she knew. I'd been a royal pain these last months, and she had taken it with minimal complaints, loads of support, and productive help even when I had resisted. Unlike my mother, who had barraged me with criticism and 'advice.' Which was the reason I'd ended up living with Cara and now refused my mother's calls and had Cara delete her messages. My mother's behaviour had thrown me deeper into self-loathing. My best friend had noticed and insisted on my coming to live with her. I needed to do something to thank her for everything she had done for me. A surprise. Something unexpected. Maybe I could think of something as we ran?

I realised then that I was taking too long to answer, so I smiled and said, 'Yep.'

She smiled back, in that way which said I was going to regret giving a positive answer, then said, 'Try to keep up.'

She took off like some speedy superheroine. Amazing that cartoon 'speed lines' didn't follow in her wake. I groaned, then forced myself to match Cara's stride. While we ran, my thoughts went to other areas of my life that had fallen by the side. I'd worked as an editor at a major publishing house. In that role, I'd attended book shows and conferences all over the world. I'd even been a guest speaker at some of them, talking about the impact of writing on culture and how certain forms of writing, such as romance, are seen as frivolous pursuits despite the tremendous impact on women, culture, and even women's rights that romance books had elicited.

The publishing company had been understanding of my situation so far, but who knew how long that would last? It had already been four months since the forced leave. A fresh wave of sadness washed over me. What had I become? *Who* had I become? Who was I? An awareness of a tight, burning sensation in my lungs pulled me from answering. If lungs could talk, mine would have begged for air, reminding me how unfit I had become after months of couch-potatoitis.

In front of me, Cara glanced over her shoulder and said, 'Come on, slow poke.'

I gasped, then tried to up my pace. How had I found this motivating? She was brutal. Aah! My lungs continued to protest, but I fought against it and convinced my brain to keep my feet moving.

After what seemed like an hour, Cara stopped at a sturdy, ancient looking gum tree at one of our local parks. I slumped to the ground at the base, lying flat on my back as I struggled to get air into my lungs. Once I felt my breathing normalise somewhat, I gasped out, 'You tyrant'.

She chuckled. 'You love it.'

You love it ...

Those words, but spoken in an insidious way, lodged in my brain and looped, as if a song was stuck on repeat. A flash of memories came shooting into my brain. Three men with their hands on me. My heart raced, making my pulse beat harder. The tightness in my lungs now squeezed so hard I thought I might pass out from lack of oxygen. I felt my eyes darting around, searching for *them*. I tried to move, but I couldn't do anything. I was frozen to the spot.

Just like then.

The memories sunk deeper within me, tightening their grip. The men ripping at my clothes, touching all over my body, saying hideous things ...

A sense of movement slipped into my consciousness. Was I moving? Or was it the world around me? Was I sitting upright? Had Cara moved me? I felt a thump on my back as Cara's voice said, 'Breathe, Neo. Breathe.'

Breathe ...

That word, said in a calm and soft way, burrowed into my brain and knocked out the previous nasty ones. A new vision formed. A different man to the others. This one had warm, bright, brown eyes. *Emerson.*

His imagined figure caught my gaze and said, 'Breathe with me, Neoma.'

I obeyed, copying the slow breaths 'Emerson' took.

Somewhere through the murkiness, I thought I heard Cara say, 'That's it. Keep taking deep breaths.'

'Not deep breaths, slow *breaths.'* Emerson had said that to me during our first session and repeated it now in my imagination. I remembered that the slow breaths were important so you could 'belly breathe' properly. As I followed the faux Emerson's breath, his image fizzled out of my mind. I understood why in an instant of insight: I'd unwittingly thought of a 'fact' about breathing. *Get your logical brain online.*

It hadn't helped. My breathing was still wrong, and my brain felt fuzzy. I didn't feel 'here.' But the fact I could think these things were a positive sign. More of Emerson's techniques returned to my consciousness: 'name three things.' *Three things I can see, hear, and touch.*

I glanced around and heard my shaky voice say, 'Tree. Swing ... silver clouds.'

'What's happening?'

I continued, unable to focus on the concern in Cara's question, 'Birds. Kids laughing. Motorbike.'

'Neo, are you okay?'

Ignoring Cara again, I focused on three things I could feel. My fingers gripped onto something soft and familiar. Remembering that movement was good, I ran my hands over it and said, 'Grass,' then I rubbed my legs with both hands, and said, 'Track pants ...' For the third item, I reached over and touched my best friend on the arm, and named her, 'Cara Justine Wales.'

After I moved my hands away, I saw my best friend staring at me in obvious confusion. 'Yes, it's me. Are you okay?'

Was I? The memories were gone. I felt like I was more myself. I narrowed in on my breathing. *Back to normal.* Then, my heart. *All good there.* My body temperature felt a little hot, but that could be from the mixture of running and being triggered into a flashback?

Refocusing on Cara, I nodded. 'I'm okay.'

Cara pushed my water bottle into my hands and ordered, 'Here. Drink.'

As I drank, and noticed my core temperature cooling even more, I knew I had gotten through another triggered experience thanks to Emerson, and he hadn't even been with me. Well ... *does being in my imagination count?*

Once I recapped the bottle, Cara blurted, 'I'm so sorry. This was all my fault. I shouldn't have pushed you so hard. I--'

There was no way I was letting her take the blame for this. She had done so much to look after me, so I cut in. 'This wasn't your fault and I'm fine.'

She tilted her head to one side, assessing me. 'Really? You look pale.'

I shrugged. 'I was born that way. Blame my Nordic heritage.'

'Not funny. You look ill and weak. You need chocolate. *Frank's* is at the end of the street. Do you think you can walk there?'

Frank's Café was the name of our favourite coffee place. The thought of the namesakes' locally famous triple chocolate mousse mud cake--yes, as divine as it sounded--sent an extra burst of energy into me.

I nodded. 'I can walk.'

'Let me help you up.'

I let my best friend guide me to a standing position and didn't complain when she grabbed my arm, wrapped it around her waist, and insisted I lean on her the whole way to the café.

Once we'd ordered and grabbed a table close to the front door, my best friend said, 'You look better.'

'I feel better.'

'I'm glad. Do you want to tell me what that was back there?'

I frowned. 'It was a flashback, or panic attack. Both?'

She shook her head. 'I mean the thing you did. You were saying the names of things, touching me, doing some weird breathing.'

'Oh, right. That's something Emerson taught me.'

Cara raised an eyebrow. 'Really? Tell me more.'

Why did I think she wasn't referring to the techniques?

CHAPTER FOURTEEN

Emerson

NEOMA'S hyperaroused reactions had drilled into my brain and enhanced the interest her case had caused. Different to the cases I normally saw––which was often women with long histories of abuse. Professional instinct told me Neoma did not have a long abuse history. Whatever had happened to her had been prolonged or multiple events close together. I don't know how I knew, but my chest buzzed with certainty at my conclusion. My other previous conclusion flashed through my brain: *it had happened at the hands of at least one man.* There were tricky gender and power issues in play that could get out of control if not managed properly. I needed to remain laser-focused during our meetings together.

Refocus on your other work now.

I nodded to myself. I had spent too much time on

Neoma's file already. Although I reached for another file, when I took a breath, I realised I was still thinking about Neoma. I crossed my arms and gave in. Seeing as my brain wanted to think about her, so be it. How often had I told my clients to 'let things be, without judgement?' I let my brain loose. The next thing it latched onto was Neoma's resistance. I hadn't met as much blatant resistance to my therapy in a while. Probably another reason I'd become motivated again.

'Do I really not have to talk about things?'

'Do I have to talk at all?'

Those questions had confirmed her resistance and had boosted the impulse to see her sooner than planned. An alarm from my phone cut into my thoughts. I knew what it was for. My daily exercise and snack break. I scheduled an hour every day to stay healthy, force myself to take a break, and clear my head. Movement was as good for the mind as much as it was for the body. I grabbed my wallet, phone, and keys, slipped on my thin black jacket, then marched off for a brisk walk. A short time later, I spied one of the cafés I frequented. Though I hadn't consciously walked in that direction, my subconscious had decided it wanted coffee. Who was I to argue with my subconscious? *You do it all the time.* I grunted at that, then made my way over to the café.

When I opened the door of the café, the sight of someone made me pause. *Was it ... Neoma?* I blinked, but when her image didn't vanish, I knew I wasn't hallucinating. She was sitting at a table with a red-haired woman. The two were laughing. I hesitated in the doorway. What was I supposed to do? Stay? Leave? Acknowledge her? Ignore her?

'Are you going in, mate?'

I glanced behind me and saw a man waiting to enter. Apologising, I stepped inside the café. When I faced forward again, Neoma and her friend were staring at me. The slight commotion had drawn the attention of several others inside the café as well. I offered a closed-mouth smile at Neoma. The look on her face morphed from shock to confusion, then she gave me a hesitant smile. *What do I do?* The indecision froze me to the spot until I saw the two women exchange words. That was my cue. Time to leave. I went to take a step backwards but hesitated when I saw the redhead stand and make her way towards me. She obviously wanted to talk to me. What if it related to Neoma? I waited.

The woman smiled before she stopped in front of me and said, 'You're Emerson, right?'

'Right.'

She offered a handshake in my direction. 'I'm Cara, the one who called you about Neo.'

Neo. Great nickname. Better than 'Trauma Guru'.

I pushed that thought away and accepted her handshake. 'Nice to meet you.'

She pulled from the handshake and said, 'I came over to ask if you wanted to join us.'

'Uh …' I glanced over at Neoma, who offered me a tentative nod.

Cara seemed to understand my hesitation because she added, 'It's okay with Neo. She wasn't sure what the protocol was for clients and facilitators interacting outside of therapy, so I offered to come over and ask.'

This *would* have been a professional conflict when I'd been a registered psychologist. Now, the boundaries were less straightforward. The situation could offer me a chance to increase the level of trust between Neoma and me and, therefore, ensure Neoma didn't pull out of our next meeting. *The way you do with Sil?* I let that comment slip away and refocused on the conversation.

'I'm not sure.' If Neoma's trauma involved an element of stalking, my presence might be triggering. 'I wouldn't want to impose.'

'Honestly, it's fine.'

I glanced at Neoma again. Her expression seemed relaxed, neither smiling nor frowning––more curious. 'All right. I'll order, then come over.'

That would give me another opportunity to assess Neoma's comfort level before I joined them.

Cara nodded. 'No worries.'

As I waited in line, I glanced at the table where Cara had now rejoined Neoma. Neoma's body language looked like it had during our first therapeutic meeting: stiff, with a hint of confidence. Hard to discern how she felt about me joining them. *Cara insisted.* I didn't have more time to debate because it was my turn to order. Once I finished, I made my way to the table.

Cara looked up at me, smiled, and patted the back of the chair next to her, and across from Neoma. 'You can sit here.'

I pulled out the chair and sat. Neoma hadn't looked in my direction since I'd been in line. She kept her gaze down. Nobody talked. That's when it turned especially awkward.

Cara came to the rescue, laughing, before saying, 'Geez. Did someone die?'

Neoma and I exchanged a glance. She offered me an unconvincing, closed-mouth, almost smile as the waitress took that moment to arrive with my coffee. I thanked the waitress and took a big sip despite the liquid burning my tongue. If I guzzled it down quickly, I could leave quickly.

When I placed the mug back on its saucer, Neoma asked in an almost-whisper, 'What did you order?'

'Coffee. Black. No sugar.'

Cara sucked in a breath. 'Whoa, that's hard core.'

I shrugged. 'You get used to it in the army.'

Neoma said, 'Rations?'

'More like the need for a quick shot of caffeine to get through the day. What about you?' I nodded at her mug.

'Latte. One sugar.'

Cara said, 'You two are too hardcore for me.'

'Why's that?'

Neoma answered, 'Cara has about twelve sugars in her coffee.'

Cara play-smacked Neoma on the hand, 'I do not! I only have five. Six max.' Though she had clearly intended it as a teasing gesture, the play-smack made Neoma jump.

Cara pulled back in her seat and attempted to hide a frown I spotted anyway. In a low voice, she said, 'Sorry, Neo. I forgot.'

Neoma shook her head. 'It's okay.'

Despite the reassuring words, I didn't need to be a trained psychologist to tell Neoma, and Cara for that matter, was upset. Was Neoma indulging in negative self-talk for having had a reaction to Cara's play-smack? Or was she wanting to talk to her friend without me there? Was she uncomfortable with me at the table? If so, it might be best to leave. Before I could excuse myself, Cara's phone, on the table in front of her, rang.

She grabbed the phone, rose, and said, 'I'll take this outside. Will you be okay, Neo?'

Neoma nodded, so Cara left. In the silence, Neoma kept her gaze lowered and made zero attempt to talk to me. Yep, my cue to leave.

After downing another gulp of too-hot coffee, I said, 'I think––'

Neoma peered up, fire blazing in her eyes, as she spat out, 'I don't need you to psychoanalyse me right now.'

Whoa. I'd only been about to say I thought I should leave. Clearly, that wasn't what she'd been expecting. The palpable anger behind her words could mean a couple of things: Neoma had been triggered, likely from the play-smack, possibly from my presence, and she could stick up for herself when needed. The reaction was positive to see. Many of my clients were too frightened to speak up. They needed extensive voice work to overcome it. Neoma wouldn't need that.

A look of regret passed over Neoma's face. She lowered her gaze and said, 'Sorry. I got carried away.'

'You don't need to apologise for saying what you want or for feeling angry. I should be the one apologising.'

She glanced up. 'What for?'

'I made you feel uncomfortable.'

'No, you didn't.' The way she said it told me she was

telling the truth. She had been upset, though. *That* was obvious. She'd already said she didn't want to be psycho-analysed, so I stepped around that by saying, 'I thought you might be upset because I interrupted your girl talk with Cara?'

Almost imperceptibly, one side of Neoma's mouth quirked up in a flicker of genuine and visible amusement; an encouraging sign. 'Girl talk?'

'I should have grabbed my coffee and left. I apologise for intruding.'

'You didn't. We invited you to join us.'

'You were being polite.'

She snorted. 'Shows how much you know about me.'

'I would like to know more about you.' The words slipped out before I was conscious of thinking them, followed by the mortifying comprehension that they had another unintentional meaning. Something more roman-tic. *Oh-oh.* I needed to make my position clear. She needed to know she could trust me to remain profes-sional. To clarify, I added, 'For instance, it's intriguing that you like apple crumble muffins.' She had one on a plate in front of her. When she glanced at it, I continued, 'Not many people like them, but they're my favourite.'

She hesitated, then said, 'You can pretend you're eating healthy with the apple, but you also get a treat with the crumble.'

I grinned. 'Exactly. You get the best of both worlds.'

She smiled, and it hit her eyes for the first time since I'd known her. The jade of her irises shimmered. *Pretty eyes.* I looked away the instant the thought from our first meeting came. It was not professional to think that. I would ensure it didn't happen again. My focus would be solely on Neoma's needs. Cara returned to the table before another awkward silence could intrude. She looked at me in an assessing manner. What was she looking for?

She must have been happy with whatever she'd concluded, because a soft smile lifted her mouth before she turned to Neoma and said, 'I have to go. That was mum.'

Neoma frowned. 'Another emergency?'

'Yep. Will you be all right to get home by yourself?'

'Yeah.'

'Okay. See you at home later. Text me when you get there if I'm not back before you.'

'I will.'

It was obvious the pair cared about each other. The realisation made me feel warm inside. Neoma had someone looking out for her. Some trauma survivors had no-one. Even one supportive person could make a massive difference in the recovery process. Despite his foibles, without Silvester, who knew where I would have ended up after the incident? My parents, too.

Cara walked away, leaving us alone. Neoma was focusing on the apple crumble muffin on her plate. I noticed then that she had been picking at it, rather than eating it, and had been since my arrival. Evidence of an anxious reaction, perhaps? I *was* making her feel uncomfortable. I had to leave this time.

Neoma spoke up a second before I opened my mouth to say goodbye, 'Cara's mum always has one emergency or other going on. She seems to thrive on drama.'

It was difficult to stop my brain from analysing people and their behaviour sometimes, but I forced myself not to. Neoma had already said she didn't want psychoanalysis to be part of this conversation. To build trust, I needed to show her I would honour her boundaries.

I tried another approach. 'My aunt was the same way.'

'Really?'

I nodded, then added, 'She passed away a couple of years ago. My life's been boring ever since, even with my mum's monthly dinner invites.'

As I'd hoped, that made Neoma chuckle. Humour was a great way to create trust and lighten almost any mood.

Neoma's expression turned serious a beat later. 'Your clients having meltdowns the first time they meet you isn't exciting enough for you?'

The knowledge in me wanted to bust out. She was trying to deflect by using faux humour. Since I was trying to honour her boundaries, I couldn't launch into a spiel about deflecting.

So, I used a softer approach. 'I didn't think you wanted to talk about that?'

She shook her head. 'I don't. Forget I said anything.'

I would respect that request, which meant I had to find another way to discover if faux-humour was a common defence mechanism for her. But she didn't need to know that yet, and my investigation on the topic could wait. All she needed to know for now was that I was on her side, she could trust me, and I would do whatever it took to help her.

With those aims in mind, I said, 'If you insist. Besides, that wasn't technically our first meeting.'

'That's true.' She hesitated one moment, then added, 'I'm actually kind of glad we met that way first.'

'Really? Why's that?'

She looked down and started a slow fidget with her fingers. Had I said something wrong or was she thinking about her answer?

The waitress approached, and asked, 'Can I get you anything else?'

'No, thank you.'

I looked at Neoma, waiting for her to reply, but she was still stuck in thought.

The waitress turned towards Neoma with a look of annoyance on her face. 'What about you, miss?'

Neoma still didn't answer. *Oh-oh.* What was going on? Did I need to be worried?

CHAPTER FIFTEEN

Neoma

WHY WAS I glad we'd first met outside of a therapy scenario? I knew part of the answer: it had made me feel more relaxed during the first session because he hadn't been a stranger. And, because I'd given him a benign nickname which had, clearly, softened my conceptions of him. *Water Guy.* But, I sensed another reason hidden behind the obvious. What was it?

Cara had mentioned during our talk in the café before Emerson's arrival how good it was that one session with Emerson had helped me more than all the other counselling sessions combined. She was right. I'd been able to successfully use the techniques he'd taught me. Was that it? His helpfulness? Maybe helping me with the water bottles had reminded my subconscious that some men could be trusted, and help for the sake of helping, and I'd liked that?

Whatever it was, I'd decided shortly before I'd seen Emerson walk into *Frank's* that I'd continue seeing him. Everything had been going well, then I'd thought he was going to ask about Cara's hand smack. I knew she had meant no harm. The unexpectedness had made me flinch. That was it, nothing to psychoanalyse. I frowned ... because there *was* something to psychoanalyse. That's why I was seeing Emerson. Why I had to continue seeing him.

'Neoma?'

The sound of Emerson's voice pulled me from my musings. I looked at him and shook my head in apology. 'Sorry, what were you saying?'

'The waitress asked if you want something else?'

'Oh, uh ...' I saw the waitress throw me an impatient look. How long had she been standing there while I'd been overanalysing everything in my mind? So much for no psychoanalysis today. 'No, that's all. Thank you.'

The woman gave us both a fake smile, then left.

Emerson looked over at me. 'Everything okay?'

I shrugged. 'Yeah, just stuck in my head.'

He nodded. I could tell he was struggling to hold back his psychobabble, like I was sure he had a couple of other times throughout our conversation. He was respecting my boundary around not being psychoanalysed, which was more than I could say about my mother.

Breaking the ensuing silence, he said, 'Thank you for agreeing to the new meeting time, too. You won't regret it.'

I snorted. 'That's exactly what someone says the moment before they make you regret it.'

He didn't respond, but looked at me like he was working something out in his mind. That made me hear how I'd *really* said the words. Not funny, as I'd intended, but cynical. A flurry of tightness hit my chest. Sometimes, I hated that I'd become this cynical, doubtful, and distrustful. I never used to be. I'd always been positive, optimistic, the life of the party ... *That woman is dead.* I looked away. Yes, she was dead, and it was for the best. That woman had gotten hurt. *Never again.* I'd had to change to protect myself. I would never make the same mistakes I had that night. I would keep my head down, mind my own business, and keep my loud mouth shut. Stay out of sight. Be boring and dull. Don't draw attention ... and stay safe.

Emerson spoke, 'Can I ask you something?'

I peeked up, curious. 'Depends on what it is.'

'Can you call me out on it if I do make you regret it?'

'Sure.'

'Shake on it?'

He moved his hand towards me. An easy-going smile lifted the corners of his mouth as he did it. Something loosened in me with that smile. I felt it in my chest. Had Emerson managed to lower my defences? Before I knew what I was doing, I'd accepted his handshake. I glanced at our clasped hands. Much like his gaze, his hand felt warm and comforting. The sensation wrapped around me, relaxing me. I peered over at him and smiled. *A proper smile. At a* man. Like the old me would have. The old me wouldn't have had a problem calling people on their crap, either, and I'd just agreed to do it again. What was happening to me? Why was I acting this way? It wasn't safe. This behaviour had gotten me in trouble. I yanked my hand free.

He either didn't notice anything amiss, or acted like he didn't when he said, 'There's something I'm curious about. Do you mind if I ask a personal question?'

I eyed him, cautious. 'Depends on what it is.'

He grinned, then said, 'What's with Cara calling you "Neo"?'

I exhaled in relief. Nothing too personal.

I explained, 'Cara thinks she's being hilarious calling me that.'

'Because of the famous movie character?'

'Yep. Sometimes, I'm not sure why I keep her around.' I rolled my eyes in a mocking way.

He smiled, warm like his hand had been. 'She cares about you.'

'I know. She's been a good friend.'

'I can see that. I'm sure you've been a good friend to her, too.'

'Ha! Not lately. Lately, I've been kind of a drag.'

'I bet that's not true.'

'Shows what you know, Mr. "I'm Such A Wonderful Psychologist".'

The words were out before I could stop them. *Ah.* I'd done it again. Me and my sarcastic mouth. My chest tightened and my brain lashed me. *Stupid. Why couldn't you keep your loud mouth shut?* I'd been so careful with men these last months. I went to apologise, but Emerson laughed before I could. The soft, easy-going tone in his laugh loosened the tightness in my chest once again. *He doesn't care.*

Once he'd finished laughing, he said, 'I'm not a psychologist anymore, and I'm sure there are sides to my practice that aren't wonderful, but I'll take the compliment.'

Was he teasing? Serious? I couldn't tell. He was smiling, but as I'd learned, smiles could mask many sins. The old me pushed at my defences, wanting to quip back at him. But the new me pushed harder. What if I got it wrong? *And got hurt.* Logically, I understood not all men were sexual predator assholes. The problem was, it could be difficult to pick the decent ones. Some charmed you with lies until they had you where they wanted you. Others could get a degree in the art of manipulation. Then, there were the mouthy ones who despised you for being mouthy right back ...

I shook my head, refusing to follow that thought through. Instead, I refocused on the current problem. Emerson didn't seem like any of those types of men. But how could I trust that conclusion? This was only my second face-to-face conversation with him, unless I also counted our meeting at the store. Plus, one phone conversation. Was that enough to get a sense of someone? Could I trust him? Could I trust *my* assessment of him? After all, I'd gotten it wrong before.

He spoke again, apparently sensing my hesitation, 'It's okay to say whatever's on your mind.'

He'd said that in our first session, too. *What's he going to do with all these customers around anyway?* Highly unlikely he'd do anything bad with a café full of people.

With a boost of courage, I released the comeback that had been sitting at the back of my throat, 'I hadn't realised I'd complimented you.'

He shrugged, relaxed. 'That depends on the way you choose to look at things, doesn't it?'

So far, so good. Better not push my luck.

'Maybe.'

To further end the conversation, I turned to my muffin, picked a chunk off, and stuffed it into my mouth. Couldn't speak, or cause trouble, if my mouth was full, could I?

Chapter Sixteen

Emerson

SHE HAD a charming sense of humour, yet she seemed to shut it down before it could gain traction. The humour added a flicker of life to her sometimes lifeless eyes, but it died too fast, as if she was ashamed of that side of her personality. Why? I made a mental note to add that to her file. Might be something there to focus on in our next meeting. *If* she showed up.

As she placed a sizeable piece of muffin in her mouth, I sensed that was a signal, whether conscious or subconscious, that she was finished with the jokes. I left it at that. She seemed somewhat relaxed, and I wanted her to stay that way. By not pushing her, it would increase the trust between us, too.

We sat, with her snacking on the muffin and me taking

small sips of my now-cool coffee. Though Neoma focused on her food, I knew from experience she would be aware if I watched her. The hyperaroused could be ultra-sensitive to the stares of others. Hence, I tried to avoid looking at her directly, focusing on the occasional glance instead. Through the glances, I noticed slight differences in Neoma's physical appearance. For one thing, the black t-shirt she wore was a little more fitted than the outfit I had seen her in at the office. Her hairstyle also looked more polished, as if she had spent more time on it than usual. I was pretty sure she was wearing some kind of lip gloss as well. If my observations were correct, these small signs were positive steps for Neoma. Was she aware of the changes she'd made? Was she feeling more positive about herself and her life? *Hmm.* That confirmed my decision towards reconnection exercises for the next meeting. If she was making changes already, it would push her a little more and increase her confidence. Most of the concern I'd felt over Neoma's therapy dropped.

I smiled, then took another sip of my coffee. She stuffed another piece of muffin into her mouth. The urge to see what else I could find out about her so I could work it into her therapy filled me up with questions. Did Neoma still work? Some clients left their jobs after trauma. Others overworked to distract their minds.

Neoma swallowed, then peered over at me, and said, 'I should go.'

'Me, too.'

My departure was overdue. We stood together and walked out of the café in silence.

Outside, I squinted at the change in light, and said, 'Looks like the sun's out at last.'

Neoma looked up, shielding her eyes from the sun's rays with one hand. 'About time.'

Then, we walked off ... in the same direction.

'Oh.' She stopped and looked at me. 'Did you walk here?'

I nodded. 'It's an easy way to incorporate exercise into my work day.'

'That's right. Your house is close by.' A frown line appeared between her eyes. She was not pleased with that recollection.

I joined some dots. Her house must be near *Frank's* as well. I'd never paid close attention to her address on the in-take form. We might be walking in the same direction for a while. Which meant ...

'You feel uncomfortable with us walking the same way together?'

She gave a quick nod in response.

'I'm happy to hang around here for a bit while you go on ahead of me.'

'It sounds stupid when you say it out loud like that.'

'It's not stupid if it makes you feel comfortable, Neoma.'

She hesitated.

'Honestly, I don't mind. You're allowed to feel however you feel and set boundaries. If it makes you uncomfortable having me walk in the same direction as you, I will stay here until you are out of sight.'

She thought it over, then waved her hand, and said, 'No. No. It's fine.'

'Are you sure?'

'Yes. Cara will feel better knowing I didn't walk home alone.' Without waiting for me to reply, she turned and walked way. Over her shoulder, she added, 'You coming?'

CHAPTER SEVENTEEN

Neoma

WE WALKED IN SILENCE. I had no clue what to say. I felt stupid––it wasn't Emerson's fault that his house was near Cara's––but not uncomfortable. Which was a surprise. A pleasant surprise. Maybe I was lowering my walls when it came to men?

Emerson broke into my overthinking, by saying, 'You have a pretty neighbourhood.'

I glanced in the direction he was looking and, for the first time since moving to Cara's, I *saw* the trees that lined either side of her street. They provided a canopy that curled over you like a protective parent.

I smiled. 'Yeah, it is.'

'How long have you lived here?'

'About seven months.'

'That's not long. Can I ask why you moved here?'

My throat choked up. Why'd he have to ask *that* question? I swallowed, then answered, 'Long story.'

I could tell by the way his gaze darted over my face that he'd sensed something more to my answer. Bloody psychologists. No, bloody trauma recovery facilitators. *He'd reminded me he wasn't a psychologist anymore.* A burst of curiosity wanted me to ask why the change in profession, but my new self didn't want to cross any lines. So I kept my mouth shut.

He nodded, showing he accepted my answer. From what I'd gathered about Emerson so far, I knew he wouldn't push for more unless I made it clear he could. We settled into a relaxed silence.

As we walked, I realised I was thirsty. The coffee and walk had probably dehydrated me and I'd thrown my used water bottle in the recycling bin at the café. Before I'd realised what was happening, I blurted, 'God, I could use a drink.'

A thinking crinkle formed across his forehead, and he said, 'I thought you said you don't drink anymore?'

An old cheeky impulse crept up on me as I quipped, paraphrasing his words to me from our first session, and hinting at our first actual meeting, 'I didn't mean alcohol. I was thinking bottled water.'

He laughed. 'Touche, using my own words against me.'

I smiled. 'Couldn't stop myself.'

'I did set myself up for it.'

'You really did. Not my fault.'

'Not at all.'

The way he said it hinted at a deeper meaning. I looked away and silence settled between us for a short distance, before he said, 'I think it's great how blunt you can be sometimes.'

That took me aback. 'You do?'

'Yes. It's refreshing.'

I didn't respond, unsure how to take that. Bluntness had gotten me into trouble, so ...

I changed the focus back to him, 'What about you? Are you a drinker or teetotaller?'

He shook his head. 'I usually don't drink much.'

Usually.

I couldn't prod further, even if I'd felt brave enough to, because he changed the subject back to me, 'Can I ask how long ago you quit?'

'About seven months.' The answer slipped out before I could stop it.

I saw him connecting puzzle pieces in his mind. He was working things out. It kind of made me angry. I could feel my body getting hot because of it. I had been assured, by both him and Cara, that I wouldn't have to talk about anything I didn't want to talk about. And yet ... it had been me who'd slipped. That thought repeated in my mind. *I* had slipped. Emerson had asked permission with his questions. He'd not pressured me. I'd *willingly* given him more information than the other counsellors had gotten between them. Why was I sharing this stuff with him? He didn't need to know. Nobody did. I felt the anger growing, making me hotter. As it did, I understood something else: the anger was aimed at myself, not Emerson. I was angry that I was allowing my guard to drop with him.

He must have noticed my agitation, because he said,

'We don't have to talk about that if you don't want to. How much further until your house?'

Ha! He was getting me to focus on facts to switch my logical brain online. *I see you, Emerson Novak.* I bet he thought he was being so stealthy. But, two could play that game.

I pointed in the general direction ahead of us, then answered, 'It's the house near the tree.'

After a half second pause, he said, 'The street is literally lined with trees.'

'I know.' I peered over and grinned.

He laughed, then shrugged. 'At least you're smiling again.'

It was true. My heart felt tingly, in a good way, with the realisation. No anxiety lingered. Only ease and comfort. *And, it's happening with a man.* That had to be a positive step in my recovery, didn't it?

We walked along in silence once more, which gave my mind time to overthink. There was no denying that Emerson had helped me. I'd been able to pull myself together after the run with Cara by using the techniques he'd shown me. This was the first time in months that I'd felt the tiniest bit in control of my life. And, I was lowering my walls and taking better care of myself–– though that still needed a lot of work. Emerson had flicked something on in me. Something I'd thought had died all those months ago. Unbelievably, I found myself *anticipating* our next session. I never would have thought that was possible.

We reached Cara's driveway, so I stopped and said, 'We're here.'

Chapter Eighteen

Emerson

NEOMA LOOKED AT THE GROUND, avoiding my eye contact as usual. I hoped the exercises I gave her would eventually help her stop doing that. She had already made remarkable progress. She was taking care of herself in small, but noticeable, ways. Her self-censoring was easing up. She was showing different sides of her personality which, based on how she tried to cover them up, told me she had hidden them for at least seven months. *Seven months.* I'd made connections to that number. It raised questions I would note down later. My heart beat with renewed excitement at the prospect of our upcoming meeting. The sensation slipped when Neoma glanced up.

The confused look on her face made me explain why I was still standing there with her, 'I was waiting until I saw you get inside safely. Is that all right, or would you prefer me to leave now?'

My parents had raised me a bit old-fashioned and, even though I was more aligned with modern norms, old-fashioned manners sometimes escaped. Some women seemed to like it. Others didn't. How would Neoma feel about it? An unreadable expression passed over her face, and I couldn't figure out what she was thinking. Her gaze drifted upwards, hesitant as it landed on mine. *That's it. Strong eye contact, Neoma.* Pride at her progress filled my chest.

As soon as I thought it, she looked away again, and answered, 'You can wait. Thanks.'

'No problem.'

She turned and walked to the front door. After unlocking it and stepping inside, she peeked out, then gave me a hesitant wave. I smiled and waved back. Then, the door closed, and she was gone. Safely home.

As I walked on, I pulled out a palm-sized notepad and pen from the lining on the inside of my jacket. While my head was still full of the details of our time together, I jotted down everything I could remember from our walk and time at the café. *What happened seven months ago to make Neoma move? And stop drinking? Why does she sometimes shut down her humorous and forthright sides, as if she is ashamed of that part of her personality? I complimented her bluntness to show her it's all right to be herself. Will she feel comfortable enough one day to be fully herself? Will she trust me enough to be vulnerable?*

We'd only technically had one meeting––not including our initial contact, and the phone call, and our time at the café, and our chat now—–but I wanted to know the answers to these questions in a way I had never wanted to know them before. Yet, she wasn't ready to tell me everything. Would she ever? Even the small snippets of information she shared with me seemed to bother her. I continued writing and felt lighter, and re-enthused, once it was all down. This was going brilliantly. The thought made me smile as I continued towards my house.

CHAPTER NINETEEN

THAT WAS INTERESTING. I unexpectedly met up with Emerson at the café after my run with Cara. He ended up kind of walking me home. It felt weird at first, but comfy after a bit. He even waited until I got inside the house ... but asked if he could before he did it. Who does that these days?! It was actually nice. Both the asking for permission (I've noticed he does that a lot) and waiting to see me go inside. If I'd had someone to do that for me on that night, maybe--

I screamed at the sound of my phone ringing. My thoughts raced in time to my raised heart rate. When I saw the name on the phone's screen, I exhaled to calm myself and snatched up my phone from its spot on my bedside table.

I answered, speaking before my best friend could, 'Sorry. I forgot to call. I'm home safe. Emerson walked me home.'

With confusion tinting her tone, Cara repeated, 'Emerson walked you home?'

'Yes.'

'I'm glad you didn't have to walk alone.'

'I thought you might say that.'

'You know me too well.'

'Ditto.'

'We *are* best friends.'

For some reason, those words stabbed my heart. Tears threatened in my eyes. Through a choked voice, I said, 'Thank God I have you.'

'Awww, thanks.'

'No, I mean it. You've really stepped up and stood by me when I needed it. You're the best best friend ever. I want to do something to say "thank you" for everything. Maybe cook you a nice dinner?'

'You don't have to do that, Neo.'

'I know, but I want to do it. You deserve something nice. Who knows? I might even invite Oscar along.'

Oscar was a waiter at *Frank's*. Cara had a tiny crush on him.

'Don't you dare, or I'll find a new bestie.'

I answered with mock-terror. 'Ah! I'll be good. I swear.'

'Yeah, right. Guess there's a first time for everything.'

I laughed.

Her voice turned serious when she said, 'It's so good to hear you laugh.'

I smiled. 'Yeah. It's been a while.'

'It has.'

Neither of us spoke, but a string of silent words passed

between us. Words of gratitude, true friendship, and acceptance.

I broke it by saying, 'It's getting too soppy now. I'm going to make a list of grocery items. How does the Hungarian beef and onion stew you love sound?'

It was her favourite dish.

Cara moaned with delight. 'Soooooo good. I haven't had that in ages.'

Which probably meant it had been a month. Cara's mother was half Hungarian and conjured it up for her daughter on a regular basis, even during her regular crises. Thankfully, she'd shared the recipe with us for those moments when she was out of town or working. In contrast, my mother made no special meals and the only thing she conjured up was criticism. She'd called again yesterday. This time, she hadn't left a message, as I'd requested multiple times before. Maybe she was finally listening?

Cara cut into my thoughts, 'Do you need me to bring anything home?'

'No, but can I ...' My intended question––can I borrow your car?––trailed off when something occurred to me. I'd relied on Cara for personal transportation these past months, because I'd left my car in the garage at the apart-ment. Time to decide whether to keep it or sell it and buy a different car. One that didn't remind me of that night. In the meantime ... 'Can I be a pest and borrow your car when you get home?'

'Of course, and you're not being a pest.'

My heart warmed. What would I have done without her in my life? I was so lucky.

Lucky ...

Wow. That word would never have escaped my mouth in the previous months. Was this all because of Emerson Novak?

CHAPTER TWENTY

Emerson

MY HEAD WAS STILL full of notes for Neoma's recovery as I neared my home, so I didn't notice Sil sitting on my bottom step until I'd almost walked into him.

Before he could say anything, I blurted out, 'Why are you here?'

He raised an eyebrow, like I was insane for asking the question. His tone matched the look when he answered, 'You called me ...'

'I did?' I reached into my pocket and found my phone. Sure enough, there was a call to Sil. I looked back at him. 'Accidental pocket dial.'

'Mmm. *Accidental.*'

Ignoring his hint at a deeper Freudian meaning to the call, I said, 'Sorry you wasted your time coming over.'

He shrugged. 'Now that I'm here, why don't you tell me what's got you away with the fairies?'

'A patient.'

'Tough case, huh?'

'You could say that.'

Sil rose, standing at the same height as me when I reached his side. His blue-eyed gaze locked onto mine, enquiring like his words that followed, 'Anything I can help with?'

'Not sure. She's ... intriguing.'

'How so?'

We walked together up the stairs while I answered, 'She seems to have, I don't know, renewed my passion for psychology or something? It's hard to explain.'

When we stopped at the top of the stairs, he said, 'I understand perfectly.'

At least that made one of us.

'You do?'

He nodded. 'We all go through slumps and plateaus in our careers. In psychology, you can spend years going through the motions, until you get that one client who jump starts your enthusiasm again.'

'Yes, that's exactly it!'

He smiled, knowingly.

The gesture clicked something into place in my brain. 'Is that what happened to you? With me, I mean?'

'Yes, Emerson. Why do you think I'm so dedicated to helping you?'

'Ah.' His agreeing to be my mentor and continued interest in my progress made a lot more sense to me now.

After all, I'd developed that same sense of dedication to helping Neoma. 'Why didn't you tell me this before now?'

'Would you have been ready to hear it?'

He had a point. 'Probably not.'

'That's why I didn't say anything. Now, tell me more about your client.'

'We'd actually met before our first session. Briefly. Outside a ... store.'

If I admitted it was outside the Bottle-O, we would get side-tracked.

'I'm sensing more to that story, but we can let it go for now. Are you worried about a potential conflict from that meeting? Because I wouldn't worry if it was a brief encounter.'

I shook my head. 'I'm not worried about that. She's displaying hyperaroused responses. Sometimes, she self-censors, but other times, she blurts out the funniest or bluntest thing.'

'I see. I'm guessing she hasn't divulged information about her trauma?'

He knew my unorthodox methods. We'd discussed it often enough. He always seemed interested in learning more about my methods. Even though he specialised in more traditional psychoanalysis, he was not so engrained in the 'old school' mentality that he was closed off to newer research.

'No, but I'm pretty sure there's an element of assault. Probably sexual.'

'Would explain the hyperarousal.'

'I'm working on developing trust and comfort

between us. She's doing well with the exercises I've taught her.'

'That's good. But, if there's a sexual element, she might be wary of men.'

'I know. I'm trying to be careful. Respecting her boundaries and such.'

'Good, good. What exercises have you taught her?'

'We started with breathing ...' I paused, realising I didn't know why Sil had come over instead of calling me back. 'Not being rude, but why are you here?'

'Can't one professional visit another professional in the field?'

'Yes, but they usually call first.'

Sil shrugged. 'I thought you called me, remember?'

'You could have called me back.'

'I was in the neighbourhood.'

'Uh-huh. You live half an hour away.' I didn't bother keeping the scepticism from my voice. We both knew what this was about. A sneak visit to check in on me. He wanted to give me the psychological lecture he'd missed on the anniversary date. I hadn't been sneaky enough myself when I'd kept our phone conversation short. *Dammit.*

He waved towards the front door. 'Aren't you going to invite me in?'

'Do I have a choice?'

He grinned, then slapped me on the back. 'Come on. It won't be that bad.'

'Promise?'

Sil chuckled. 'I promise nothing. You know that.'

I did. It was his famous motto. *I promise nothing, but*

that doesn't mean you shouldn't talk to me. I questioned that line of thinking every time I was about to be on the receiving end of his talking. My ex-psychologist was a big believer in 'talk therapy.' Again, I had nothing against it, the practice helped lots of people. It just hadn't been helpful for me or some clients who came to see me. Regardless, I drew in a slow breath to prepare for the upcoming lecture, pulled the front door key from my pants pocket, and welcomed Sil inside.

Once we settled in the lounge room with coffees––*yes, I needed another if I was going to sit through the inevitable lecture*––and chocolate biscuits, I looked at Sil and said, 'All right, lay it on me.'

He turned his body to face mine, his expression serious before he said, 'I know I say this every year, but I'm hoping if I repeat myself enough, you'll finally listen: you *need* to face what happened to you.'

'I have faced it.'

'How?'

'I look after myself on the day.'

'By running to alcohol, pills, and random women? That's not self-care; it's self-destruction.'

'It's one night a year, and there wasn't a woman this time.'

Did he notice I didn't deny the involvement of the other two in my ritual?

'That one night could destroy you and everything you've tried so hard to build.'

I shook my head, refusing to accept that. 'This works for me. It's evidence-based practice.'

'It's evidence that numbing yourself for eight years

doesn't work.' I winced when part of me acknowledged some truth in that statement. 'If I was still your official psychologist––'

'I guess it's lucky you aren't my psychologist then.' I'd raised my voice and immediately regretted it. I knew he was trying to help, but he wasn't. I exhaled and ran a hand down my face. 'I apologise, but you know talking about it hasn't helped me.'

He waved his hand, dismissing my apology. 'I know you don't wish to talk about it, but please, find a therapist you can work with.'

'I don't have time.'

'Excuses, Emerson.' I frowned, knowing what he meant. *Those in denial make excuses.* He continued, 'I'll write you a referral. It can be someone in your field. Whatever it is, I'll do it. You need to find a therapy that works.'

'I *have* found a therapy that works. Why do you think I do the work I do?'

He sighed. 'For someone who specialises in trauma, you have a glaring blind spot.'

'What blind spot?'

'Yourself. You teach your clients these amazing techniques, but you don't use them *fully* yourself. You––'

I cut him off. 'I do use the techniques.'

'I emphasised the word "fully."'

'I use them fully.'

He raised an eyebrow. 'When was the last time you "connected with life" by going out with a friend or family member?'

'I'm with you now.'

'I'm not a friend or family member, and we haven't left your house, so it doesn't count. Who else have you been out with lately?'

'I go to Mum and Dad's for dinner once a month.'

'Correct me if I'm wrong, but those dinners used to be weekly. What else?'

Did hanging out at the café with Neoma and walking her home count?

No. She's a client. What about my regular meetings with Jack? Nope. Business associate. *Dammit.* Sil had a point. I hated when that happened. Still, it didn't have to mean anything. I'd been busy. My practice was getting more bookings and Jack's publicity took up the rest of my time.

In a neutral, non-judgemental tone, Sil asked, 'Why didn't you accept the tickets for the rugby league? You could have taken your dad, or a friend, or a date, with you.'

That question hit me in the chest, forming a guilty lump. How long had it been since I'd been somewhere with Dad, or Mum, beyond the dinners? How long since I'd called a friend, let alone gone out with them? Newt, my best friend, had gotten married *five months ago* … Had it really been that long since I'd seen my best friend? Had to have been even longer since I'd been on a date. *Double dammit.*

With a mixture of guilt and clinging denial, I answered, 'I was working. I told you that. I thought you understood.'

'I *do* understand. More than you do right now.'

Annoyed now at his continued pushing, and what I felt

to be a patronising remark, I snapped back, 'Stop psycho-analysing me.'

Whoa. Yep, I'd heard it: I sounded an awful lot like Neoma's response to me in the café ...

'I will when you take responsibility for your life.' His tone was still neutral. I'd always wondered how he managed that. He was frustrated with me, but a passer-by would never have been able to pick it.

That fired up my frustration even more and came out in my response, 'I *have* taken responsibility. You saw me after I got back. I was a wreck. But I pulled myself up. I built a successful practice. I have offers coming in. I should be signing contracts soon.'

'More things to keep you distracted from the truth.'

'What truth? That I drink once a year to get through a difficult time? This is getting tedious.'

'I agree. It's tedious that you continue to drink to numb yourself and your emotions. Come on, Emerson. Somewhere in that magnificent brain of yours, you know it won't do you any good in the long term. You need to face your emotions.'

I shook my head. 'That's not the only way. We know so much more about trauma therapy than when you originally studied it; no offense.' When he indicated with a wave of his hand that he'd taken no offence, I added, 'Logic can keep your brain and reactions stable.'

He sighed. 'In some cases, yes. But "logic" has made you put up walls to keep people out. Literal walls. Like the screens you use in your therapy, and the phone calls you make to clients––'

'I do that to make them feel safe!'

Despite my exasperation, Sil's tone remained calm when he said, 'Does it keep them safe, or *you*? It seems to me like you've recreated the safety you felt on that day by barricading yourself away.'

I could almost feel my brain wanting to switch to the past at his triggering words. In response, I looked away, forcing my brain to name physical objects around me. *Mat. Television. Biscuits.* I needed my logical brain online so I wouldn't slip back to that day, and also to calm the emotions taking over.

Sil distracted me by saying, 'You tell your clients that they need to "reconnect with the world," all while you shut yourself off from it, and them.'

'Don't use my own words against me, especially when it's out of context.' I'd filmed an entire professional web series on reconnection, thanks to Jack's business contacts who'd helped with the lighting, sound, and filming. It was part of the therapy I was planning to use with Neoma. Nobody knew reconnection like I did.

'I'm worried about what will happen if you keep going this way.'

'I've managed perfectly well so far.'

'You haven't managed, you've coped. There's a differ- ence.' How the hell could he remain sounding so calm? If I wasn't so aggravated, I'd have asked.

I exhaled, loud and long, then reached up to my fore- head. It throbbed the way it had the day of my first meeting with Neoma. 'You asked me to find something that helps. It's helped. What's the problem?'

'The problem is you are engaging in negative coping mechanisms and you can't see it.'

We were going around in circles. The same way we did every year. 'Silvester––'

'What about the sleeping pills?'

I froze. *Damn. He must have noticed my lack of denial about the pills and alcohol earlier. What should I tell him?* He'd caught me with the pills a couple of years ago, and I'd told him I'd never use them again. I opened my mouth to deny using them, but I saw him read the truth in my face.

'Emerson … you know better than this.' He shook his head. Disappointment from an authority figure could be so cutting, even when they weren't your parent.

'I'll stop.'

He caught my gaze in a locked stare. 'You sound like an addict.'

I know. I'd heard it, too. Was I in denial? My head throbbed harder in response. I rubbed my hands over my temples, not wanting to think about any of it right now.

'Can we talk about something else, please?'

Sil looked at me with still disapproving blue eyes, but said, 'For now.'

CHAPTER TWENTY ONE

Neoma

HE WAS behind the screen again. What was up with that? I understood his explanation for it, but it felt off. It wasn't the full truth. At the same time, I had to admit the screen provided an easy-going anonymity with it; like a confessional in church. I refocused on what he was saying.

'Many psychologists believe post-trauma responses result from a perceived threat to life, but I think it's actually the result of a perceived threat to your *ideas* about life. Mainly that you are safe and in control of what happens to you.'

I nodded. 'Makes sense.'

Both ideas had been upended within me.

'Glad to hear you say that because today is all about reconnection therapy.'

'Which is?'

'Which is about reconnecting with life and the world around you.'

'I thought breath was life.'

He laughed. 'It is, but reconnection is also life. Having said that, we always start with the breath. Would you take some slow breaths with me?'

'Sure.'

I followed his instructions––breathe in to a four count. Hold for two. Exhale on a five count. Hold for two––even though I knew them well, having practised the breathing for over two weeks now. I closed my eyes as he instructed and let the soothing sounds of his voice lull me into a relaxed state.

'You can open your eyes whenever you're ready, Neoma.' I opened my eyes as he asked, 'Do you feel relaxed?'

'Yes.'

'Fantastic. I'm going to ask you some questions, but you don't have to answer out loud or tell me anything. Thinking about it in your head is fine. Does that sound all right with you?'

'Yes.'

'Great. I want you to think of at least three positive, happy memories from your life so far.' *Positive and happy memories.* Not many lately. 'You don't have to rush. This isn't a timed exam.'

Good to know, because I was sure this would take time.

'You ready?'

'Yes.'

'Let me know once you've thought of them.'

I let my thoughts wander. *Positive. Happy.* The first memory that popped up was a holiday I'd had with my parents at the Gold Coast in Queensland. We'd visited all the major theme parks. My mother's behaviour had fit in with the childish, fun vibe at the parks and my father had let me get everything I wanted at the gift shop. They had spoiled me that day and I'd loved it.

I smiled at the memory, then refocused. *Positive and happy.* The day I met Cara. Our first day at uni. We'd literally bumped into each other when we'd been rushing to our classes. Our books had flown in all directions and we'd landed on the concrete on our butts. We'd looked over at each other, locked eyes, and burst into laughter. That had bonded us instantly.

I felt my smile deepen. Now for a third memory. *Something happy and positive.* The day I'd achieved my goal of hiking up a popular mountain in thirty-three minutes. It typically took forty-five minutes, according to the sign at the bottom. The sign had also said one hiker had made it up in thirty-five minutes. Cara had made a flippant comment, 'Bet you couldn't make it up in thirty minutes.' I'd been determined to prove her wrong. Cara had been flabbergasted when she'd met me at the top ten minutes later. She'd said, 'Why aren't you that motivated during our runs?' I'd been stretched out on the ground, hacking my lungs up, and unable to stand on my jelly legs, so I hadn't been able to say, 'Because you don't tell me I *can't* do that'. I'd forgotten how much I could thrive when challenged.

I opened my eyes and said, 'Wow, that was easier than I thought.'

'That's wonderful to hear. The point of that exercise is to get you focused on good memories. Trauma survivors can get stuck in a loop of negativity and negative memories. Having several good memories to cling onto in the darker moments can be a useful tool. Try to think of happy memories if you get stuck in a negative loop. Do you think you could do that?'

'Yes.'

'I want you to think about something else now. Your friends. When was the last time you went out with a friend? Again, you don't have to answer out loud.'

I'd gone for another run, and café visit, with Cara before coming to the session.

'I went out with Cara this morning.'

'Someone other than Cara?'

Damn. How long since I'd seen my other friends? I thought back. It had been my birthday party. *Seven months ago ...*

I spoke so the thoughts wouldn't come, 'A while ago.'

'What about your family? When was the last time you spoke to an immediate family member?'

My throat gripped at the thought of my mother. It had to be at least six months. I was an only child, and with my father's death three years ago, there were no other immediate family members. My heart ached at the thought. I missed my father sometimes. He would never have let me live with Cara, insisting I stay with him and my mother. And he would have gagged my mother's insensitive reactions.

Emerson must have realised I wasn't going to answer

that questions aloud, because he continued by asking, 'How about any extended family?'

My aunts and uncles lived all over the country, so we saw each other once a year, at Christmas, when we had a big family get-together. It was the beginning of October now, so that meant it had to have been around ten months since I'd seen any of them.

'What about work colleagues or study partners?'

Again, it had been over four months since I'd spoken to my boss. Not since she'd put me on forced leave. Part of that had been her insistence. She'd said I should call 'when I felt better'. Part of it was shame and embarrassment. Who didn't remember making a spectacle of themselves at work? Crazies, that's who.

'What about hobbies? When was the last time you did something you love?'

Did the run with Cara that morning count? Probably not. It wasn't exactly a hobby or interest, and I wouldn't put it in the 'something I loved' category. Running was more for the fitness benefits, so I could play volleyball with enough endurance and stamina. *Volleyball.* I'd loved that once. And my career. My job had been such a major passion at one time. I loved working with books and authors. Reading. When was the last time I'd picked up a book and *really* read it? Too long. *You cooked dinner for Cara.* Yes, I did. That was something I loved, too.

'Can I ask if any of those questions prompted answers?'
'Yes.'
'Yes, I can ask, or yes, they prompted answers?'
'Both.'

'All right. Can you think about the answers you gave? Pick something you might want to change. Make sure it's something that involves interacting with other people. Someone other than Cara.'

Someone other than Cara.

'Do you think you can do that?'

'No.' It came out sounding panicked. I knew why. The last time I'd gone out with other people, it had ended with me being hurt. The night *it* had happened, Cara hadn't been able to meet me until later. Her tardiness had saved me in the end. She had intervened, scared the men off. Since then, she had become my figurative lifeline. The one person I felt completely safe with.

'Do you mind me asking why?'

'Yes.'

'All right.'

The simpleness of that response annoyed me. How could it be 'all right'? Nothing about this was right. First, he had no clue what I'd gone through. *To be fair, you haven't told him.* Second, he was behind a blasted screen, so how could he see if everything was all right!

'Are you ready to continue?'

'No.' It came out huffy.

He paused, then said, 'Do you want to talk about it?'

'No.'

'I understand.'

That angered me even more. I felt it flare up inside my stomach, tightening into a ball. How could he understand?

Before I knew what was happening, I heard my voice

snap at him, 'I don't think you do understand. How can you?'

Another pause. *Oh, no.* Had I stepped over the line?

'You're right. I don't understand. I didn't mean to offend you, or make light of your experiences, I was trying to support your decision not to talk.'

I knew that. Of course, I did. It wasn't even him I was angry at. Not really. It was the situation. The fact that one major event had changed my life to where the thought of going out with anyone besides Cara filled me with anxiety and dread.

'It's not fair.'

'No, it's not.' His tone was the soft, soothing one I liked. I sighed as he continued, 'Whatever happened to you, Neoma, you didn't deserve it and it wasn't fair. You know that, don't you?'

I nodded, but realised he couldn't see me behind that stupid screen, so I said, 'Yes.'

'Good … would you take some breaths with me?'

'Sure.'

It would help to calm me down. I followed his instructions again.

Finished with the breathing, he said, 'Can I run you through a vital signs scan?'

'Yes.'

He kept his tone low and soft. It was easy to relax when his voice sounded like that. I focused on each of the vital signs––heart rate, breathing, temperature––all were fine.

'How do you feel now?'

'Better. Thanks.'

'Not a problem. Why don't we take a break?'

Muffled sounds of a chair pushing back over carpet echoed from the other side of the screen. Soft footfalls came next. Then, Emerson peered from behind the screen. His face had a concerned expression that reminded me of the way Cara looked at me sometimes. Like I was broken or defective. I hated it and wanted to tell him to stop, but I'd already had an outburst. Instead, I bit the words away and looked down. When I tried to swallow, my throat felt choked up.

'How's your throat?'

My head flicked up in shock. *How does he know?*

My eyes must have asked because he explained, 'All that vocal expression can make your throat sore, especially if you've gotten used to keeping what you want to say to yourself.'

I nodded, then realised he wasn't offering me a drink. Isn't that what you did for people with sore throats? Basic manners.

Again, I think he saw that thought spread over my face because he said, 'It's all right to ask for what you want and need, Neoma.'

I hesitated. Was he going to make me ask for a drink? That seemed a little childish.

'Please, tell me what you want.' His tone sounded encouraging. He wasn't trying to play a childish game. This was him trying to help me speak up.

I swallowed and found my throat had opened. 'Could I have some water, please?'

He didn't answer--ironic considering he'd badgered

me about using my voice--then walked to the bar fridge
in the kitchenette opposite his desk.

Chapter Twenty Two

Emerson

My heart had reached out to her, knowing she was upset about whatever had happened to her. Then, seeing the way her face had changed when I looked at her from behind the screen, the expression had told me she'd wanted to say something but had stopped herself. I felt frustrated when she self-censored. I preferred when anger overtook her. Even when displaced, because at least it was honest. Real. I knew I was glimpsing the true Neoma at those times. That's why I'd encouraged her to speak now. To stop the self-censoring.

Focusing on the present, I opened the fridge door and grabbed a bottle of water. She accepted the water with a quick, 'Thank you,' so I went back around the screen and plonked myself down on the chair behind my desk. The sound of Neoma uncapping the water filtered through the screen and Sil's words flashed into my mind. *Logic has made you put up walls to keep people out. Literal walls. Like the screens you use in your therapy* ... A pinch of doubt crept into my mind. Was he right? Now wasn't the time to be pondering the answers.

I refocused, cleared my throat, then asked, 'Do you feel ready to get back to our meeting?'

'I think so.'

'In that case, can I make a suggestion?'

'Depends on what it is.'

My mouth nudged up at the corners. This was one of her sayings. We all had them, the common phrases we used.

'If you don't want to reconnect with an old friend, how about someone new?'

'You mean a stranger?'

'It doesn't have to be. It could be someone you've interacted with, or seen around, but don't know well. An acquaintance.'

'Oh, no. That's even worse.'

'Can I ask why? You don't have to answer.'

'*Why?*' Incredulity dripped from the word. 'Are you sure you're a trained psychologist?'

I heard her clap her hands over her mouth. *Self-censoring.*

'I'm sorry, I--'

I stopped her from finishing the apology by bursting out with laughter.

In a tentative tone, she said, 'That's ... funny?'

'It is.' I put amusement into my voice to keep her relaxed and stop her slipping into a hyperarousal reaction.

She hadn't responded, so I added, 'Someone I know would love you. He thinks I have room for improvement, too.'

'Pfft. Don't we all? Anyway, who's he to judge?'

'A professor of psychology with a thriving professional practice.'

'Oh, wow.'

'Tell me about it.'

'He doesn't sound very nice.'

'No, he is. I'm mad at him at the moment, so I'm being harsh.'

'Why are you mad at him?'

It might have been simple curiosity, but I sensed the real motive behind the question. An attempt to switch attention from her and onto me.

'Nice try. We're focusing on you.'

'Damn. Nearly had you.'

I laughed, enjoying her sense of humour.

'You have a nice laugh.' The words were low, almost as if she'd said them to herself.

'Thank you.'

Women had complimented me on my looks, body, and personality before, but this was a first-time compliment on my laugh. Strangely, it felt more intimate than the physical compliments had been, but not in a flirtatious, seductive, or inappropriate way. A subtle tingle passed up my spine. Seemed I enjoyed unique compliments.

'Ah … where were we? You said no to acquaintances.'

'That's right.'

'Can I ask if you're working now?'

'I'm on leave.'

'I'm guessing work colleagues would be a "no" as well, then?'

'You guess right.'

My mind searched for a solution. 'In that case, why don't you go out with Cara? But somewhere you don't usually go together. Not Frank's. Somewhere other people will be as well. Can you agree to that compromise?'

'I can.'

'Fantastic. We have the task nailed down for our next meeting. Would you also––'

'Wait. Who said anything about a next meeting?'

No. I thought I'd done well at increasing our trust and therapeutic connection. I'd even thrown in an anecdote about Sil for that purpose. Yet, she was still having doubts. I tried to keep my tone neutral when I asked, 'You're having doubts about returning?'

She laughed. *Laughed.* I noticed her laugh sounded nice, too.

She stopped laughing to say, 'I'm coming, but I couldn't resist. You were sounding so serious.'

I grinned. 'Not funny.'

'Why are you smiling then?'

I glanced at the screen. Could she see me? Didn't seem to be any holes.

'How do you know I'm smiling?' I leaned over my desk, getting closer to the direction of the screen. 'Are you psychic?'

'Ha! Hardly. I heard it in your voice.'

'Is that so?'

'Mm-hmm.'

A comfortable silence passed, and I was sure I felt a subtle shift in the aura between us. She was learning to trust me. *Maybe you are learning to trust her, too?* Pushing that thought away, I returned my attention to Neoma. This had to be a positive step forward for her. I had to keep that momentum going. What was the next best step in helping her? A simple idea came to me.

Chapter Twenty Three

Neoma

IN A MORE BUSINESS-LIKE VOICE, Emerson said, 'I want you to continue practising the exercises you've learned so far, plus, when you get home, I want you to write down the memories you thought of today in your journal. That way, you can go back to them if you need to. Can you do that?'

'Yes.'

'I also want you to note down at least three positive experiences you have before our next meeting in your journal. It can be something small, even if it's noticing a pretty flower. It doesn't have to be earth-shattering. I want your brain to get accustomed to noticing good things in your life. Do you think you can do that?'

'Yes.'

'Great. We'll have a lot to go over in our next meeting

then. Speaking of, can you come back in a fortnight? Same day and time?'

'Sure.' I didn't even need to check my calendar. Nothing else demanded my time.

'That's booked in ... I'm sure you and Cara will have an adventure together as well.'

'We'll see.'

'Do you have any questions before we finish up?'

'No.'

'In that case, I think we can stop there for today.'

As I hopped into my best friend's car a short time later, a new resolve settled over me. *I think it's time to sell my car.*

Chapter Twenty Four

Emerson

As I CLOSED the front door behind Neoma at the end of our meeting, I heard my phone buzz with a reminder alarm. *Great.* What had I forgotten? I returned to the home office and grabbed my phone from the desk. The reminder which had popped up on my screen read: Dinner at Mum and Dad's. I groaned and noted an immediate impulse to cancel. At the same time, the memory of my conversation with Sil returned. I *had* pushed our formerly weekly dinner catch-ups to monthly. I'd spent the day convincing Neoma to connect with others. Shouldn't I take my own advice? Besides, I hadn't had a proper, long conversation with them since last month's dinner. I had to go. Resigned, I went to the bathroom to shower.

* * *

Mum looked over the table at me and asked, 'How's the practice coming along?'

I swallowed the piece of chicken schnitzel in my mouth, then answered, 'I have a new client, and I'm so impressed with her progress. Honestly, I'm not sure I've had anyone else come as far as she has in such a short period of time.'

Although I was no longer professionally obliged to adhere to the psychological code of conduct, I still believed in the merits of the code. That was why I kept the details vague and didn't mention Neoma's name or the fact she was a trauma survivor.

'You seem quite … enthusiastic … about her.'

I nodded at Mum's words. 'I am. She's really renewed my passion for therapy.'

'I can see that.'

My parents exchanged a look, loaded with meaning.

I was about to ask what I was missing, but Dad said, 'That's great news, Bud.'

Hmm. There was definitely something in his tone. And, Mum's eyes seemed to be … sparkling. She also looked like she was trying to suppress a smile. What was going on?

Before I could speak, Dad added, 'What's this woman's name?'

Mum play-smacked Dad on the arm, reminding me of the incident between Neoma and Cara at the café. 'You know you can't ask him that, Murph.'

Dad raised a hand in a show of apology. 'Sorry, sorry. I can't help my curiosity sometimes.'

An image of Neoma and her unnecessary apologies came to mind as Mum scolded, 'Well, help it and mind your business.'

The way she said it …

I lowered my fork to the table and asked, 'What's going on?'

Dad shook his head. 'Shirl and I are just happy for you, Bud.'

'We are *so* happy for you, Ems.'

I smiled. 'Thanks.'

Looking back at my plate, I scooped up some peas mixed with my dad's famous cheesy paprika mashed potato and popped it into my mouth. The smoky, salty, savoury flavours combined on my mouth. *Mmmm.* Why had I stopped coming around every week when I could get food like this again?

CHAPTER TWENTY FIVE

ONE WEEK LATER

Neoma's journal
Entry #13

Positive experience: the bees I saw in the garden while watering the flowers this morning. There'd been something intoxicating in watching their little flower-to-flower dance. They knew who they were, what they wanted to do, and had no shame in buzzing around, taking as much nectar as the flowers wanted to give. No shame. No guilt. Pure purpose. Good for them.

I read over the words in my journal to double check for anything else I wanted to add. Nothing else came. The task Emerson had assigned, of writing down positive experiences, had been fairly easy. Like he'd suggested, I focused on the small things in my life. They added up when you paid attention, which was probably the point of the exercise.

I smiled at that and closed my journal just as Cara knocked on my bedroom door and asked, 'Ready to go?'

I looked down at the outfit I'd put on before sitting down to journal: a new, bright yellow crop top with matching tank top and black leggings. Yes, I was ready.

Chapter Twenty Six

Emerson

THOUGH I WAS on the phone with Neoma, for our between-meetings phone call, I could tell from her tone that she'd been in the middle of doing something. Why did I seem to have a knack of interrupting her? It was the café all over again.

I sat back in my desk chair. 'You sound busy. I can call back.'

'Don't hang up. I need an excuse!' Her tone was low and urgent this time.

I scrunched my forehead, concerned. 'Is everything all right?'

'Yes, just on a run with Cara ... she can be a real ball breaker.'

I couldn't help the laugh that came out. *She has a way*

with words. 'I'm sure she can be. In that case, I called to check in with you. How have you been since our last meeting?'

'Fine.'

'Can I ask if you've had a chance to go out yet?'

'Not yet. But Cara's been scheming all week, so I have no doubt it'll be something over the top.' And, with the easy humour she let herself indulge in when her guard was down, she made me let go of concerns I had interrupted her for a second time.

I laughed. 'Whatever it is, I hope you enjoy yourself.'

'I doubt I will, but I'll do my best to pretend.'

Even with the hint of amusement behind her words, I frowned. She was deflecting by using humour again.

Keeping my voice low so my words wouldn't come out sounding harsh, I said, 'Don't do that. Be yourself, Neoma. It's better when you're being true to yourself.'

She quietened, and I wondered if I hadn't changed the tone in my voice enough. Or sounded too judgey. Too preachy? But then she said, 'Thank you.'

The slight croak in her voice hit me in the stomach. 'I hope I haven't upset you.'

'You haven't.'

'I'm glad.'

'Me too …' A moment of silence passed. I felt a soft, odd tingling in my chest at the same time as Neoma said, 'Cara's making signals for me to get off the phone. I'd better go. See you next week.'

We said our goodbyes and hung up. I started making notes in Neoma's file. She was making wonderful progress. One of the fastest I'd ever had the pleasure to witness, which only added to the initial excitement I'd felt about her case. In response to the thought, my chest expanded with happiness. I finished the notes in her file and finished for the day. As I left the home office, a thought came: *What will our next meeting bring?*

Chapter Twenty Seven

Neoma

On my skin, I could feel the sheen of sweat, a combination of running with my best friend and the low cloud coverage had produced. Cara and I stepped into *Frank's.*

Before I could take a step towards the counter, Cara said, 'I'll order. Why don't you grab a table?'

A slither of suspicion crept up my spine. What was she up to? Her face showed a coy smile. *Hmm.* Flirting with Oliver, perhaps?

Grinning, I nodded and left her to her seduction. Sitting alone a moment later, I thought about the check-in call with Emerson. He'd encouraged me, saying it was okay to be who I am. I'd gotten emotional during the conversation because I'd had so many people tell me parts of my personality were defective. Especially my mother.

After she'd found out what had happened to me, her first words had been 'I warned you that mouth of yours would get you in trouble one day'.

Cara, my late father, and now Emerson were the only ones who'd assured me it wasn't wrong to be 'mouthy' and 'opinionated.' I'd been told for so long it was wrong, including on *that* night, which is why I'd curled in on myself and become this shell of a person. I'd shut down and unplugged from life. Even though it felt clichéd to think, Emerson had shown me how to plug back in and open up to myself and my life.

At the thought, my overanalysing brain kicked in. Was the progress real? Was it too soon to feel this way? Was it all in my head? Was I making it all up? This could be some kind of placebo or beginner's luck? What would I do if none of this worked in the long-term? Would I be this way forever? As questions continued to overwhelm my mind, I realised my breathing had sped up. I tried to slow it down using the slow breathing technique Emerson had showed me, but it didn't work. The growing panic made my heart race in time to my breath, making my chest tighten. I closed my eyes and tried to focus on my breathing again. *It's not working.* If nothing changed soon, a full panic attack was coming. *In the middle of the café.* That thought fuelled the panic and blurred my brain. What was I supposed to do? All the techniques I'd been shown locked themselves up and refused to give me access. My chest squeezed. *I can't breathe.* I reached for my throat as my mind whirled. *What's happening?* When I opened my eyes, everything looked closed in around me, suffocating. *I need to get out of here.* But how? Nothing looked right. *Where am I?*

The moment it felt like I might pass out from lack of oxygen, a soothing voice cut into my mind—*you're safe, Neoma. I know you're confused, but try to focus on my voice.* Emerson's words during our first therapy session seemed to shift something in my chest, softening the grip of panic. I drew in a slow breath as more of his words came. *Try to think of happy memories if you get stuck in a negative loop.* This situation wasn't entirely in context with that, but what did I have to lose? It was the only thing my brain could grasp.

I closed my eyes again. *Happy memories* ... the first time I'd heard Emerson laugh replayed in my imagination. The sound seemed to shimmer through my cells, dissolving the panic in its wake. I opened my eyes. *I'm in the café.* More aware now, I turned my attention back to breathing, taking in several slow, calming breaths. I looked down and saw my hands shaking. *Just breathe.* That was all I had to focus on right now. I followed the four-two-five-two pattern for several more cycles before I felt relatively settled.

With my brain clearer, I scanned the café for Cara. What was taking her so long? My gaze landed on her, at the side of the counter. She was chatting with Oliver. The way she leaned into him ... yep. Suspicion confirmed. Flirting. At the thought, Cara turned and walked back to our table. She had a strange smile on her face—like she was busting with excitement but didn't want to show it. I rubbed my hands over my legs; movement to release excess panic from my nervous system.

Cara plopped herself into the seat opposite mine then said in a whisper, 'Oh my Goddesses, Neo.'

'What?'

'Oliver just asked me out.'

'Oooh, what'd you say?'

'I said "yes," of course!' She paused and looked at me in a way that hinted at mischief. What was she up to? Before I could ask, she continued, 'Remember Oliver's friend Raj?'

'Vaguely.'

He had dark hair, dark eyes, and a dark complexion. *Almost the exact opposite of Emerson.*

Her eyes sparkled with mischief. 'He wants to go out with you.'

'What?'

Cara grinned. 'Don't look so surprised. You know you're gorgeous.'

'Pfft.'

Had she seen my hair lately? Yes, I'd been putting more effort into it, but it was still a basic effort of brush-and-go. Same for my makeup. I'd been sticking to tinted sunscreen, lip gloss, and concealer. Nothing dramatic. Nothing to turn a man's head.

Cara's expression turned serious. 'You *are* beautiful, Neo. Look at you. You're one of those annoying, naturally stunning women.'

I shook my head. 'No, I'm not.'

She reached over and took my hands in hers. We'd both noticed the increase in my tolerance to her touch. 'I hate that your self-esteem has suffered and I'm even more convinced this will be for the best now.'

The way she said it had my intuition pinging. '*What* will be for the best?'

Cara waggled her eyebrows before answering, 'Oliver suggested a double date with Raj.'

I pulled away. 'He what? No.'

'Why not? You said you needed to go out with me before your next session with Emerson. This would be perfect.'

Damn. Yes, I had agreed with him to go out and do something different with Cara before our next session together. This fit into the different category. I would also have something to tell Emerson when he asked about it, and I could write something more interesting in my journal than watching bees in the garden. From memory, Raj was good-looking. He'd also seemed polite and somewhat quiet the two or so times I'd met him. Not loud or threatening in any obvious way. My instincts signalled a green flag with him. And, if my instincts proved wrong, Cara would be with me. She wouldn't let anything bad happen to me. *Just like she'd saved me that night.*

'Please, Neo.'

'Fine. I'll go.'

She squealed and clapped her hands together. 'I'll go tell Oliver the news.'

CHAPTER TWENTY EIGHT

Emerson

NEOMA SEEMED DIFFERENT. More confident, but also more guarded. How was that possible? I jotted a note in her file, then refocused on the purpose of our meeting. We'd gone over her use of the exercises and journaling, both of which she'd assured me were going well. She'd also admitted to using the 'happy memories' exercise to stave off a panic attack. It made me feel warm inside to know I was helping her. In the almost seven weeks I'd known her, I'd witnessed a noticeable change. Neoma had become more confident, seemed better able to handle some of her more troubling trauma symptoms, and was engaging in life again. Which reminded me …

I glanced toward the screen and asked, 'Did you go out somewhere new with Cara?'

'Actually, I did.'

Did I detect a note of excitement in her tone?

'Can I ask what happened?'

'We went on a double date.'

'A double date?' I heard how my tone raised at the end, showing my surprise. When I'd suggested she do something different, a double date had been the last thing on my mind. Still, if it helped her, this was good.

Neoma continued, 'It sounds a bit old-fashioned, but I liked it. I felt safer with Cara there.'

'I can understand that.' Someone with a sexual trauma history involving men would feel safer with someone they trusted present in a potential romantic scenario. *Romantic scenario.* My stomach swirled with the words. Why did the term make me feel nauseous? Was it possible I felt … *no.* I was worried about her. That's all it meant. I forced the nauseated sensation down then turned my attention back to Neoma.

She asked, 'Do you want to hear more about it?'

The shock of her offering information to me made me blurt what I hoped was an easy-going, 'Of course.'

'His name is Raj. He's an architect. We went to a fancy French restaurant, a little too fancy for me, but the food was delicious, and we had lots to talk about.'

'Sounds like you had a fun time.'

'We did.'

'That's great to hear. Do you think you'd be up for another reconnection task before our next meeting?'

'It's funny you ask … Raj asked me out to brunch this Sunday.'

'Did you agree?'

Why did my question sound strained?

Neoma didn't seem to pick up on it. Her voice sounded even when she answered, 'I did. Does that count as a reconnection task?'

'It does.'

She continued, 'He's texting me the details of the place for us to meet up. I didn't feel comfortable having him pick me up, even though he knows I live with Cara, and could find me if he really wanted to.'

Interesting phrasing. I had so many questions, but knew not to ask. Especially not while Neoma was in a sharing mood. I didn't want to close her down when she'd just opened up. I had to give her enough space to decide how much she wanted to share and not push with too many intrusive questions. *Honouring boundaries*.

'You don't have to say or do anything that makes you uncomfortable.'

'I know. Thank you.'

I sensed silence was my best response.

It took about five minutes before she spoke again, in a quiet tone, 'I moved in with Cara after ...' When she trailed off, I thought she would leave it at that, but she added, 'After I was attacked.'

Attacked. The word sent a flurry of images through my mind. I felt my skin heat with growing fury at each possible scenario. The desire to know what had happened wrapped around my chest and squeezed. My brain fought the sensation until I thought I might explode. What exactly did she mean by 'attacked'? The question lodged in the back of my throat. I knew I couldn't ask. I had to give her space, support, and safety. If I limited my questions, I would be able to offer her that.

I closed my eyes and gave a simple response, 'That makes sense.'

She would have felt safe with her best friend close by.

'I couldn't live in my apartment anymore.'

Why not?

I bit that question down and settled on a non-invasive sounding, 'Oh?'

'The attack happened at my apartment. Intruders.'

Intruders, *plural*. I drew in a breath. So many times, I'd thought about selling my house to buy an apartment and lease an office space because I'd assumed apartments were less likely to have unwanted visitors––sometimes, ex or new clients showed up unannounced. How wrong I'd been. There were so many things I wanted to say to her then. So many questions I wanted answer to: how badly did they hurt you? How did you survive?

Where can I find the bastards?

I forced calm into my voice and said, 'That must have been terrifying.'

'Not the most fun I've ever had … anyway, I'm not sure why I told you that.'

'I'm glad you did.'

Sort of. The lingering anger, not so much. The knowledge that she trusted me enough to open up like that, absolutely.

'Thanks for listening. And not judging me.'

Why would I judge her? More importantly, that comment implied someone *had* judged her. Who? Anger fired up in me again.

I inhaled to cool myself down, then said, 'I hope you know I'd never judge you?'

'I think I do, actually.'

'That's good to hear.'

It meant I'd achieved a level of trust between us that would aid in her recovery.

Another moment of silence passed between us, then she said, 'Can I ask you something?'

'Anything.'

'How can you tell if a man's interested in you?'

'You think Raj isn't interested?'

'I'm not sure, that's why I'm asking.'

I hesitated on the corresponding question that came to my lips.

'What? I can sense you wanting to say something, just say it.'

Had Neoma turned into me?

I grinned at the thought.

Then, after a moment of lingering hesitation, I blurted out, 'Are you interested in Raj?'

'Again, not sure. Help.'

I chuckled at the mixture of confusion and humour in her tone, and was about to give my opinion when another idea struck. A different type of reconnection therapy. 'Can you go to the bookcase for me, please?'

'Okay ... I guess that's the end of that conversation?'

'It's not. Trust me.'

Oh-oh. Loaded words. Trust. Me. They'd come out before I'd been able to think about their possible effect on Neoma.

I relaxed when I heard a muffled noise--had to be her footsteps--followed by the words, 'I'm here.'

The words hadn't bothered her, and also hinted at her

subconscious trust in me. My chest almost puffed out in clichéd pride with that knowledge.

'All right. Have a look at the romance novels and pick one you think you'd like to read.'

'Is this the romance novel portion of my therapy?'

'It is. I want you to read whichever book you choose between now and our next meeting. Make notes of anything you think signals a man's interest in it.'

'Oooh, very clever, Water Guy.'

I laughed then retorted back, 'Have you chosen one, Water Woman?'

'Water Woman?'

'You're not the only one who made up a nickname that day.'

'I think we have too much time on our hands.'

I exhaled a sigh. 'I wish.'

'Clients keeping you busy?'

'Yes, especially those who keep trying to change the subject away from them. Have you found a book yet?'

The sense of a soft smile in her voice flowed through the air when she answered, 'I have, but I'd still like to hear your opinion about the ways men show interest.'

'It's basically the same way a woman shows she's interested. He'll want to know more about you, give you compliments, and ask you out. You'll know where you stand with him. On the other hand, if he's playing games, or not interested, you'll feel confused or ignored.'

'Got it. Confused or ignored means he's not interested. That makes everything clear.'

'Does that mean you think Raj is interested?'

'He asked me a ton of questions on our date. He also

told me I looked beautiful. And, he asked me out again. That means he's interested, doesn't it?'

'Sounds like it.'

Why did I frown with those words?

'I mean, the date went well, too.'

The date went well. 'Well' wasn't a word someone excited about their date would use. Did that mean she wasn't attracted to him? Or, was this a trauma response? Neoma could be keeping her walls up and not getting too invested in a man. After what she'd just confessed about her trauma history, it was a high possibility. In subsequent meetings, I would need to check if she was acting from a trauma response with Raj.

For now, I said, 'Can I ask what you mean by "the date went well"?'

'He was … nice.'

Nice. Another of those throwaway words. Was she into this guy or not?

'Meaning?'

'It wasn't as scary as I would have thought a couple of months ago.'

That comment shifted my focus. It hinted at something important, so I asked, 'Does that mean you think you've made progress?'

'I do. Don't you think I have?'

'Absolutely.'

Even though she said nothing, I could tell she felt proud of herself. As she should. The emotion penetrated the office, filling it with a lightness that had been missing for a while, but which I hadn't noticed until that moment. The next instant, my brain zeroed in on a specific part of that thought. *Emotion.* I knew better than to let my emotions rule. Emotions got people hurt. Emotions stopped someone from acting when needed. Emotions hadn't helped me stay hidden and get everyone out that day eight years ago. Logic had.

That's not completely true ...

I stood up and paced, hoping the movement would shift my logical brain back online. But it was too late. A memory flashed into my mind. The gun––

'Everything okay?'

That should have been *my* question to Neoma. Who was the trauma recovery facilitator here? I tried to respond, but found I had nothing to say. Why couldn't I speak? *The gun was aimed at––*

No. Had I spoken it or thought it? Either way, I didn't want that memory. I tried to shake my head, adding movement any way I could. It didn't work. When I tried to take a step forward, I couldn't. I had lost control and couldn't find a way out.

Just like that day ...

'Emerson?'

The room in my field of vision started to spin.

Keep it together. Keep it together. Keep it together.

'I'm getting worried, Emerson. Are you okay?'

My ribs seemed to close in around my lungs, squeezing them free of air. I choked, desperate for air. I leaned over, using my hands to hold me somewhat upright by placing them on my desk. *Breathe.*

'I'm coming behind the screen, okay?'

I still couldn't respond. Footsteps neared the screen. A familiar face peered around at me.

'Emerson!' Neoma's voice sounded distorted, as if playing back on a slow speed on a recording device.

I blinked, and she was at my side.

Her hand touched my arm. 'Emerson, look at me.'

I wasn't conscious of having moved, but I was staring into her jade-green eyes, so I must have.

'Emerson, what's my middle name?'

My mouth still wouldn't form words.

She took a step closer to me, placed her hands around my upper arms and forced my gaze to stay locked on hers as she said, 'Focus on me and tell me my middle name.'

Her middle name? What was it? My brain was not co-operating.

She persisted, 'You must know it. Cara filled in the paperwork I signed before coming that first day, and she thinks it's hilarious, so I know she would have put it on the form. Try to remember reading it and tell me what my full name is.'

The memory dashed forward. I *had* read it on her paperwork ... and chuckled about it.

My throat opened enough for me to say in a near whisper, 'Neoma Seoma Alban.'

'That's right. My full name is Neoma Seoma Alban. Hilarious, right? Let's laugh about it together.'

A tight, forced laugh echoed through my section of the home office. Neoma's laugh. *She has a nice laugh, too.* Even when it was fake. The absurdity of the situation made me join in, either consciously or subconsciously. I think mine was more hysterical at first, but as we continued laughing together, it became more natural.

Eventually, I realised her hands were still on me. *This*

could be seen as unprofessional. Move away. Maintain distance. Stay safe. My logical brain was back in charge. I stepped away from her, releasing her hold as I did, then turned my back so I didn't have to look at the damage I'd caused with my idiotic meltdown. *God, how unprofessional.*

I was grateful my tongue still worked enough for me to say, 'I'm so sorry. That shouldn't have happened.'

'A flashback related panic attack is nothing to be ashamed of, Emerson.'

Panic attack?

I spun around. 'That wasn't a panic attack.'

She arched an eyebrow at me and crossed her arms in front of her. 'I've had enough to know what they look like, and that sure looked like one to me.'

I shook my head. Why would I have a panic attack? I hadn't had one in years. I'd gotten control of myself. I'd learned about getting the logical brain online and hadn't had one since. *Your emotions have been coming out lately.* I couldn't argue with that. Hadn't my excitement at having Neoma as a client come through several times? I'd even thought about the positive feelings that had permeated the office moments ago. That didn't mean this had been a panic attack, though. It was … an emotional wobble. *Yes. That sounds logical. Does it?* Why did my brain have to fight me sometimes?

I lifted a hand to my head as a new wave of dizziness overcame me. 'I need to sit.'

Neoma rushed to my chair and pulled it out. 'Let me help.'

She reached out in a protective gesture when I

wobbled before plonking myself into the chair. When I peered up at her, worry had etched over her face.

'I'll get you some water.'

Before I could reply, she was off and at my bar fridge. She returned moments later with an uncapped bottle of water.

'Here. Drink.'

I lifted the water to my lips and gulped with relish.

'How do you feel now?'

The concern in her voice relaxed me. 'Better.'

Except, now that my head was clearing, I understood the full impact of what had happened. I'd had some sort of wobble *in front of a client.* Not just any client, either, but the client who had brought back the enthusiasm I'd first had for my career. This was bad. What was I going to do?

I pushed my chair back and stood. In a tone as stable as I could force, I said, 'Thank you for your help. I appreciate it, but I think we need a break.'

'Of course. Would you like to go for a walk around the garden to get some fresh air? I can stay here or go with you?'

No way. I had to get Neoma out of here. Physical distance meant emotional distance. That's why the screen had been put in place. *The screen she bypassed to come and help you.* Sil would have a field day with the symbology of that, wouldn't he?

Refocusing, I said, 'Actually, I think it's best if we end the meeting for today.'

'Oh. Okay.'

She sounded upset. I couldn't help it when my gaze darted to her face to see for myself. A clear look of rejection floated in her eyes. Guilt surged in me at what I was doing. I was abandoning her when she needed me the most, all because of my own idiotic lack of emotional control. None of this was her doing. In fact, with my brain fog clearing, not only did I feel embarrassed, but I also felt like I was an impostor. *I* was supposed to be in charge, in control. Hell, I was supposed to be the expert! How could I punish her for my idiocy by telling her to leave? I was supposed to be helping *her*. Instead, I'd forced her into an awkward situation––having to get me through a stressed reaction.

That couldn't happen again. It *wouldn't* happen again. I would need to think of ways to recoup the power balance, trust, and comfort this episode must have damaged. I also needed to recover the physical distance between us. Maintain professional distance and safety. But, first, I needed to take care of her needs. She was upset because of my actions.

Before she could turn away, I added, 'I apologise for what happened, Neoma. I'm embarrassed. It's nothing to do with you. I hope you know that.'

She offered me a comforting half-smile, and I saw the rejection melt from her eyes. 'You don't need to feel embarrassed. I've done much worse in front of you.'

'That's kind to say, but not true. Thank you for being so understanding.'

She shrugged. 'Eh. No biggie. See you in a fortnight.'

Somehow, I mumbled, 'See you then.'

Moments later, I heard the front door close.

Alone, I slumped back into my chair and groaned. How the hell was I going to fix this monumental stuff up?

CHAPTER TWENTY NINE

Emerson

I'D PICKED up my phone and called Sil almost before I was conscious of doing it.

As soon as he answered, a tumble of words spilled out of my mouth, 'I think I'm in trouble. This silly thing happened, and it was so unprofessional. She had to help *me*. What must she think? She seemed okay when she left. But--'

'Take a breath, Emerson.'

'Sorry, I'm panicking.'

Panicking. Panic attack ... fuck. Had Neoma been right?

'Just breathe.'

I did, but it was too fast.

'And another. Slower this time.'

I took a slower breath, the way I taught my clients.

'One more. That's it. Now, who are you talking about?'

'Neoma. The client I was telling you about the other day.'

'What happened?'

I exhaled, long and loud. 'I had a … wobble … in front of her. In our meeting. About five minutes ago.'

I was still blurting out disjointed sentences.

Thankfully, Sil took it in his stride. 'What do you mean by a "wobble"?'

'I don't know. It might have been a slight … panic attack?'

I went into a little more detail, including the part where Neoma had to come around the screen to help me.

After a pause, Sil said, 'This is a good sign.'

I scoffed. 'How can this possibly be *good*?'

'It could be a sign that you're ready to face the trauma properly.'

I sighed. 'Not this again. I called for help, not a lecture.'

'You're going to get both. First, the lecture. Even though this is a good sign for your healing, there's a high chance more intrusive memories and other post-trauma symptoms will come forward now. Including more panic attacks. You need to tread carefully. That is where I can help.'

'Finally.'

'Don't be cheeky. Do you want my advice or not?'

'Go ahead.'

'Stop the face-to-face sessions with Neoma.'

'What? I can't abandon her when she––'

'Let me finish. You can still have therapy sessions with her, but do it over a video link or phone call. I think if you limit the physical contact you have, the symptoms will be more likely to even out.'

'But——'

'You might be too emotionally invested in her recovery to the point that it's affecting your own mental health.'

'I thought you said the wobble was a good thing?'

'It is, but it's also put you in a tricky situation, psychologically. You have to look out for yourself. Self-care, remember? If you maintain the physical distance, you can maintain your therapeutic obligations and protect yourself.'

'Wait, I thought you didn't like me keeping my distance from clients? You gave me a whole lecture about the screen. Didn't you say it keeps *me* safe?'

'This is different.'

'How?'

'Neoma has reignited your enthusiasm for psychology. As such, you're emotionally invested in her recovery. That caused you to lower your mental and emotional defences, meaning the time was ripe for your brain to make you deal with your own repressed trauma. You had a "wobble", which led to Neoma crossing your emotional-slash-physical wall——' I knew Sil would have a field day with the symbology of that. '——Meaning you are now more vulnerable to further post-trauma symptoms. Especially in Neoma's presence, since your brain is clearly aligning her with safety for you. How'd I do?'

'Sounds about right.'

I'd been doing well. Then, Neoma Alban had dropped water bottles near me. It was almost as if I had been splashed with that water, and it had woken me from a deep sleep. I couldn't ignore reality any longer. *Dammit.* Why'd Sil have to be so annoyingly right all the time?

'Then, listen to me when I tell you to stop the in-person sessions for now.'

'For how long?'

'Until you can be sure that your trauma symptoms have stabilised.'

'All right. Thank you, Sil. I appreciate your advice.'

'I'm just pleased you knew you could call me and did.'

I smiled. He had my best interests at heart. Like I did with Neoma. But, taking care of myself would help Neoma's recovery as well, so that's what I had to do. No more in-person meetings for now.

A yawn escaped my mouth. *Ugh.* 'I'm feeling the after-effects of the panic attack now.'

'You'll feel better after a sleep.'

No arguing with that. Which was an all too familiar situation when it came to my ex-psychologist. Most of the time, that bugged me. But not today. Today, I was beyond grateful to have him in my life. Even more so because he hadn't brought up the topic of me seeing another thera-pist, even though it was the *logical* next step. My brain had kicked back to logical mode for me to be thinking that.

Which is why I said, 'Hey, Sil?'

'Yeah?'

'Next time, can we talk about that referral to one of the therapists you were telling me about?'

'I would love that. In the meantime, get some rest. You sound like you're about to drop dead.'

In response, I yawned again.

CHAPTER THIRTY

Neoma's Journal
Entry #18

SOMETHING HAPPENED in my session with Emerson today ... and I think it might have shifted the dynamics between us. Everything was going as usual, then he went quiet. I called his name, but he didn't answer. I kept calling and heard nothing, but then these whimpers came from his side of the screen. I got worried. The urge to check on him came over me, but I hesitated to go behind the screen because it felt like I would be intruding on his personal space. I hate my personal space being intruded upon. So, I called his name again, and he still didn't answer. That was when I got really worried, and that over-rode the 'intrusion fear,' and I went behind the screen to check on him.

I'm glad I did because what I saw was not good. He said he didn't have a panic attack ... but I know he did. He basically shoved me out the door after it, saying he was 'embarrassed', which is probably partly true, but I think it's more than that. After the attack, I pushed people away and tried to stuff my *feelings down however I could. Nothing worked, and in the end, here I am in therapy, learning ways to deal with the fallout that crappy night caused.*

You know, I even told Emerson some of it today. I couldn't believe it. The words blurted out. We'd been talking, and it felt natural to tell him. You know what I think it was? He's never pushed me for details. Everyone always wants to know the details. What business is it of theirs? Are they masochists? Did they want to see me get upset? I couldn't understand the appeal other people found in hearing the misery of other people's stories. Emerson hadn't done that. I'd felt supported and unpressured. I know I'm making it sound like no big deal. It was. I didn't even tell him the main parts. There is no way I've dealt with all the feelings from that day, and I'm not ready to talk -- or write--about some of that stuff, but I've come a long way, and I'm not in the same head space that I was.

Maybe that's why I could see the truth on Emerson's face? Still, I didn't push the point. I know from experience that being too blunt about it would only strengthen the denial. He needs to reach the point I did after the incident at work had made it impossible to deny the attack had affected me. That's why I'd decided to leave it. But, I must admit to being curious. Isn't he some wonderful therapist? Why is he having panic attacks? Is he in therapy himself? Not that any of that is my business. I just can't help the curiosity about him. Anyway, I went on the date with Raj. I'm not feeling anything beyond friendship, but I'm not giving up yet. What can you guess about your potential future with someone after one date? Nothing. So what if there are no 'sparks'? Chemistry could develop from friendship. All I had to do was give him a chance. A real chance. We have a brunch date arranged in three days, so I'm going to wait and see how that goes. Maybe I'll look into his eyes and feel different? Maybe I'll gain some clarity after reading this romance novel Emerson asked me to choose as part of my therapy exercises this fortnight?

The sound of my phone ringing pulled my attention from the journal. I glanced at its position on my bedside table, noting the name that came up on the screen. Mum. I wrinkled my nose and ignored the call. After it went to voicemail, I waited, but no beep signalling a message came. *Hmm.* That was the second or third time she'd called without leaving a message. Maybe she was finally learning to respect my boundaries?

Even though I wanted to believe that, her unthoughtful behaviour after the attack had me cautious. Especially now I was feeling more like myself than I had in months. One conversation with her could throw me off track. I didn't want to take that chance. I felt a smidge of guilt slither through my stomach. My father would hate what had happened to us.

I looked up at the sky outside my open window and whispered, 'Not yet, Dad.'

First, I needed to get stronger to face my past. Then, maybe I could face my mother.

CHAPTER THIRTY ONE

Emerson

I WAS SITTING at my desk in the military base, prepping for an emergency client who was due to see me the following day, when I realised I needed a fresh client file. I went to push the intercom button on my desk phone to ask my assistant, Emory, to get a new file for me. As my hand touched the button, I remembered Emory was on leave for the day. Like I was supposed to be. With a groan, I pushed myself upright, walked out of my office door, and made my way to the file room behind Emory's desk in the waiting area. I used the card on the lanyard around my neck to buzz myself into the classified area. I wasn't in there long before I heard a muffled noise coming from the direction of the waiting room. The sound made me pause. Was someone here? Maybe another emergency client? Or, had Emory shown up? *Turning around, I stopped when I heard an angry voice say, 'Where is he?'*

A scared voice answered, 'I told you, he's got the day off today.'

I went to take a step forward, but a loud 'crack' *froze me to the spot.* What was that? I listened again.

The first man said, 'Liar. My wife said he'd be in today.'

'He's not here. You can see for yourself. That's his desk.'

Are they talking about Emory? What is this about?

I stepped towards the door, which had dark one-way glass. Through it, I could see a man I didn't recognise: tall, solid, with a crew cut––even without a uniform, he screamed 'army or military.' There weren't many civilians like me on the base, so that was even likelier. The man had a gun in his hand ... aimed at another man's head. The other man wore an army uniform, and he was on his knees in front of Emory's desk. I couldn't see his face, so I wasn't sure if I knew him.

My heart thumped in my chest as every action slowed down. What is happening? What should I do? *There was no phone in the file room and I'd left my mobile in the office.* No computer back here. *I had no phone or internet to contact anyone. I glanced at the back left of the room, where the emergency exit was located. It set off an alarm when activated. If I used the exit to find someone to help, the gunman would hear the alarm. It could tip him over the edge and make him shoot the other man. That wasn't an option.*

I had no way to contact anyone or leave to get help.

I was trapped ... yet also relatively safe.

Nobody knew I was in here. Emory and I were the only ones with card access, so nobody could get in. Nobody from outside could see me because of the darkened glass. All of that had to work to my advantage somehow, didn't it? My thoughts were cut short by the door to the waiting room flinging open.

Someone I recognised—Harry. My boss, who was close to retirement—walked in and said, 'Are you here, Emer——'

Harry stopped what he was saying when the gunman spun around, aimed the gun at him, and barked, 'Close the door!'

My boss obliged, then was directed to join the man on his knees.

Once settled, Harry said, 'What's going on here?'

'I'm asking the questions. You came in looking for that Emory bastard, which means I'm right, he is here.'

Harry shook his head. 'I came in looking for Emer ...' He hesitated, then looked around. His gaze went to the room I was in before he looked back at the offender and finished, 'Yes, I was looking for Emory.'

My boss saved my ass. Never was I more grateful for having a similar name to my assistant. It had been a point of annoyance for some time for both of us. But not today.

'Where is he?' The gunman's face had grown red from visible anger.

'He was here a moment ago.' Harry reached for the phone on Emory's desk. 'I'll call and see where he is—'

'Stop that!' The gunman whacked his gun over Harry's knuckles, sending a familiar cracking sound through the room. The previous crack must have been him hitting the other man with the gun. *That conclusion made me shudder.* Why was the man so angry? What was his problem? What did he want?

My boss rubbed his knuckles, then said, 'I'm trying to help you, mate.'

'I'm not your mate. Especially if you're buddies with that bastard.'

'Why don't you put the gun down and tell me what Emory's done? We can sort this without anyone getting hurt.'

The gunman scoffed. 'You really think I'm that stupid? Just like my stupid bitch wife. She thinks I'm an idiot as well. She didn't think I'd figure out she was fucking that bastard behind my back.'

I sucked in a breath. The separated woman Emory had said he was seeing. This was the husband. From memory, Emory had said the man was abusive and had a temper. Shit, shit, shit. The longer this goes on, the worse it will get.

I rubbed a hand through my head. What do I do? My heart was beating too fast for me to come up with a plan. I couldn't stay in this room like a coward ... but I would be in danger if I made myself known. What would happen to everyone if I went out now? I was the only one who knew what was happening. Few people came into this office. Myself, Emory, and Harry were the key staff. There was an on-call psychologist for when I was on leave, but she wouldn't come on base without being called in. I would have been notified of any impending visits from her, too. The cleaning crew came after hours. Other than that, there were clients, most of whom lived on base ...

My mouth felt dry as a new realisation sunk in.

Clients. Some of them popped in without notice to book another appointment or change their times. Please, do not let a client come in now. At the thought, the waiting room door opened. The gunman didn't notice; too revved up on adrenaline. But I did. So did Harry and the other man. My heart rate sped up in both fear and excitement as I saw one of my clients, Marshall, draw his own gun and shout, 'Put the gun down.'

The gunman turned. In what felt like slow motion, I couldn't do anything as I watched a bullet leave his gun. Bang!

The gunshot in my nightmare startled me awake. I jolted upright, opened my eyes, and scanned my surroundings. I was in my bed. My breathing was too fast and I could feel sweat beading on my forehead. *Just a dream.* I wiped my forehead with the back of my hand and exhaled in a slow breath. My heart was still beating too fast. I reached toward the glass on my bedside table, took a big gulp, then returned the glass to its former spot.

I'd had a nightmare. That realisation made me frown. I'd gotten on top of the nightmares years ago. Sil had warned me this could happen. I got up to pace. Movement was good. As I walked to discharge the nervous energy and get my logical brain back online, something occurred to me.

So many variables had happened that day. I shouldn't have been in the office, for one thing. It had been my day off, but I'd gone in to prepare. What would have happened if I'd stayed at my home on the base instead? *They all would have died.* That's what everyone had said at my bravery award ceremony. I still didn't think I deserved that thing. I hadn't behaved bravely by hiding away in that room while they suffered. My brain, too emotion-choked to do anything useful. *Not true.* I frowned, fighting my head. Acting at the last minute, after the gunman had left the room, to get everyone out the exit, thereby, setting off the alarm and stopping the gunman coming back, didn't count! Waiting until it was safe to act was what cowards did.

I shook that thought away and continued pacing.

Another question came. What would have happened if I hadn't gone into the file room? I'd thought about that decision so many times. *Walking into the file room.* That was the thing that had saved me from the horrors I could have experienced. That one act. Even after years of experience with trauma, it still surprised me how often one act, one decision, one moment could change your entire world. Mine had never been the same. Those men and their families would never be the same. All because of one violent man's psychotic break and jealous rampage. No matter what people said, the knowledge that the man was in jail did *not* help. It didn't stop the nightmares, the flashbacks, the questionings and requestionings. It didn't stop the 'what ifs' and 'maybes.' It didn't stop the guilt or shame. *Coward.*

I shook my head. It was no use giving into these emotions, it only drew out the symptoms and made me feel shit. Sil had been right. Getting some physical distance from Neoma would be good for me. She had been forcing me out of my logical mind too much. As a result, my nightmares had started up again, and I'd had a panic attack. As soon as it seemed like a decent time to call, I would change our meeting to a video call. This would be best for the both of us. I couldn't help her if I kept getting emotional and having trauma reactions.

Chapter Thirty Two

Neoma

I HAD BEEN OBSESSING over Emerson's panic attack since our session three days ago. He hadn't called like he had between our other sessions yet. Once more, the urge to call and check on him filled me up. The usual question that accompanied that urge returned: is it appropriate to call him? Maybe if we'd been friends. Maybe not, seeing as we were client-trauma recovery facilitator. The probability of that stopped me from tapping his number on my phone. Besides, there was plenty of time for him to call until our next session. Even so, I checked my phone, and still saw no missed calls or texts from him.

'Honestly, Neoma. If there's somewhere you need to be, we can do this another time. It's no problem.'

'Huh?' I looked over the table at Raj. 'What did you say?'

'That's the third time you've checked your phone. Is there somewhere you need to be or … is this your subtle way of telling me to get lost?'

'What? No. Nothing like that.'

We were on our brunch date and I could see I had been appallingly distracted.

Raj sent me an interested look, then leaned across the table, getting closer to me. 'What is it like, then?'

I placed my phone back in my bag and smiled. 'It's nothing to worry about. What were you saying before? Something about your job?'

He nodded and said a string of words that entered my ears but didn't reach my brain. My thoughts were still on Emerson. Was he okay? Should I call to check in on him?

The questions looped until Raj snapped me out of them by saying, 'Speaking of jobs, have you received a return-to-work date?'

On our last date, we'd skimmed over the topic of my 'leave of absence.' I'd been grateful to have Cara with me. She'd deftly managed the question and moved the topic on. No mention of the real reason for my leave had been made. Cara had spun it out, so it sounded like a sabbatical rather than a forced probation situation due to the crazy way I'd apparently behaved.

I shook my head. 'Not yet.'

'You aren't getting antsy? I think I'd get cabin fever without something to do beyond housework.' He lifted his hands like he'd realised he might have said something offensive, then added, 'Not that there's anything wrong with that if that's what you want to do.'

I was about to answer with what had become my automatic response: no, I wasn't antsy. But the words wouldn't come out. They didn't seem authentic. That made me pause and ponder. Was I ready to return to work? Probably not full-time, not straight away, but part-time was a definite possibility.

I looked at Raj. 'You might be right. I think I am getting antsy.'

He gave a quick nod. 'You seem like me. The sort of person who can get things done when it's needed.'

'I was.'

His forehead crinkled. 'Was?'

'Yeah. I kind of ... lost that. Hence, the sabbatical.' It was sort of true. 'I think I'm ready to get back into it.'

He smiled. 'That's great, Neoma. I hope it works out.'

'Me, too.'

We settled into a companionable conversation for the rest of our brunch date.

Afterwards, as we stood out the front of the café, Raj turned to me and said, 'What would you say if I asked you to dinner sometime next week?'

What would I say? I wasn't feeling a connection beyond friendship with Raj. But he was polite, knew how to keep the conversation going, and wasn't pressuring me to move fast. I glanced up and noted the contours of his face. Yes, he was handsome, but it didn't make me *feel* anything.

I could hear Cara in my head saying, 'Give him a chance,' like she had before I'd left.

So, I looked into his eyes and said, 'Okay.'

He exhaled in a sign of relief then smiled. 'Thank you. How about I walk you to your car?'

I nodded. When we reached the driver's side door of Cara's car, Raj didn't try to kiss me. He simply opened the door and held it while I stepped inside. *See*, Raj was respectful. He didn't pressure or push. He seemed happy to go at whatever pace I set. I needed to give him a proper chance.

Before he closed the door, he said, 'I'll call you to set up a date.'

'Okay.' I tried to sound excited, even though I didn't feel it.

Then, I drove away. By the time I turned into Cara's driveway, I'd decided to call my former boss and discuss the possibility of returning to work. But first, I wanted to run the idea by Cara. I found her in the kitchen and ran it past her.

She nodded. 'I think part-time's an excellent idea, Neo.'

Something in her tone that made me say, 'But?'

'But I think you should bring this up with Emerson. See what he thinks before you go ahead with it. Your bosses might want a medical certificate from him, too.'

Crap. She was right. I hadn't thought about the medical certificate. Seeing as I'd had a meltdown or breakdown at work, they would want to cover themselves and ensure I was ready. Calling Emerson would also give me a legitimate excuse to check in on him, too. Decided, I thanked my best friend and walked to my bedroom to make the call. I pulled the phone from my bag just as it rang. Glancing at the screen, I saw an unexpected name. *Emerson*. He was calling to check in on me while I was calling to check in on him. *What a synchronicity!*

After introductions, I said, 'I have something to run by you.'

'All right.'

He sounded tired. Had he not slept well? Should I ask or mind my own business? That was the boundary that had plagued me my whole life. When was it 'right' to let my big mouth go and when 'should' I muzzle it?

'You know you can say anything you want to me, Neoma.'

Had he sensed my unspoken thought?

I cleared my throat and said, 'I was thinking you sound tired.'

'I am, but I'll be fine, and I'm guessing that's not what you wanted to discuss.'

'No. I was … thinking about going back to work.'

'That's amazing news.'

'It is?'

'Isn't it?'

'That's what I'm asking you.'

'Do you feel ready?'

'I think so.'

'But do you *feel* so?'

'I'm not sure.'

'All right. How soon were you thinking of going back to work?'

I shrugged despite his not being able to see it. 'I only had the idea this morning, so I haven't had a chance to go over all the details, other than starting back part-time.'

'I agree part-time would be best for now.'

'Do you think I'll need a medical certificate from you?'

'You might. If you do, let me know and I'll write one up.'

'Does that mean you think I'm ready to go back?'

'I do, but it's how *you feel* that matters more than my opinion. That's something we can work on in the next meeting.'

'I'm confused. What is it that we can work on?'

'Your feelings.'

'My feelings? I thought you were all about the logical, not the emotional.'

'Emotions and feelings aren't necessarily the same thing.'

'And it's my feelings that need work?'

'I think so, yes.'

I couldn't help myself. With purposeful cheekiness, I quipped, 'But do you *feel* so?'

He laughed. 'Yes, I feel so.' I grinned to myself before he changed the topic again, saying, 'How have you been going with the exercises?'

'Good.'

'Any questions, thoughts, concerns?'

'No.'

Only about dating Raj. Which, for some reason, felt weird to discuss with him.

'You've been journaling and practicing the exercises?'

'I have.'

'Have you been able to write some positive experiences in your journal?'

'I have actually … and not all of them were about bees.'

'Bees?'

'Long story. Not important.'

'In that case, I have something to run by you.'

'What is it?'

'I was hoping you would agree to an online video chat for our next meeting?'

'Online? Why?'

'It works better with my schedule.'

That wasn't the real reason. I could sense it. Even so, the conclusion didn't alarm me because my intuition told me something else: he had a good reason for the decision. Maybe because he still felt embarrassed? I decided now was not the time to push him on it. We all deserved our privacy. I hated it when people pushed me about topics I didn't want to discuss, so I agreed without a fuss.

I was about to say goodbye when he said, 'Neoma, I want to apologise again for … the way I acted during our last meeting.'

'It's fine.'

'Thank you for being so understanding.'

'You've been understanding of me.'

I thought I sensed him smile before we said our good-byes. The possible smile must have transferred to me, because when I walked out to find Cara in the lounge room, the first thing she said was, 'I'm guessing that grin means Emerson gave you the green light?'

I nodded. She jumped up from her spot on the lounge chair and ran to me.

'That's amazing news. I'm so proud of you.'

'I couldn't have done it without your support.'

'Pfft. Of course you could have.'

'No, I don't think so. You don't realise how much I've depended on you these past months.'

'You've been there for me plenty of times.'

'Not like this.'

She shook her head, denying her role. I couldn't understand it. 'Why won't you accept my thanks?'

She frowned, then looked down. 'I …'

'What is it?'

She peeked up. 'I feel like I let you down that night.'

'What? Why would you think that?'

'If I'd told work I had to leave early, and come to the party, instead of saying I'd meet you at your place later, I could have been with you the whole time, and stopped anything from happening.'

'You *did* stop them.'

If she hadn't shown up when she had, who knew what those assholes would have done to me?

She shook her head again. 'I mean, I might have been able to stop anything from happening. They might not have tried to get into the apartment if I'd been there with you. Safety in numbers and all that.'

The way she looked at me, with such guilt, stabbed me in the heart. She'd been holding this in for months.

'Cara, I don't blame you.'

'I know, but *I* blame me. I wasn't a good friend to you that night. It was your birthday, and I bailed.'

'You had to work. I understood then and I understand now. You weren't to know what those guys would do. This isn't your fault.'

Tears were streaming down her face now. 'I'm so sorry I wasn't there.'

'Oh, Cara.' I pulled her in for a hug. That made her sob

harder. 'It's been so long since you've hugged me properly.'

'I'm sorry about that.'

She laughed through the tears. 'Look at us sorry cases.'

'Pathetic, right?'

She laughed again, then pulled away to look at me. 'Totally pathetic.'

I smiled. 'Feeling better now?'

'Yes.'

'Excellent, because I was thinking about how perfect ice-cream would be right now.'

'It's like you read my mind. But first, you should make that call to work before you can overthink it.'

Crap. I'd forgotten about that. A rumble of nerves shot through my stomach. What if they said 'no'? What if I'd stuffed up too much? What if I'd been replaced?

My best friend smiled and said, 'They'd be crazy not to take you back. I can stay while you make the call, if you want?'

'I'd like that.'

She pulled me in for another hug and I realised how much I'd missed this closeness with her. What else had I been missing out on?

CHAPTER THIRTY THREE

Neoma

I STARED at Emerson's face over the computer video link. It was a different type of screen to the one he had in his home office, but even with his face visible, the effect was oddly the same: a subtle hint of distance between himself and his client. Was it a mood he sent out on purpose, or was it subconscious? Either way, *why* did he do it? On the wall in his background, I noted a painting of a woman with a fan covering her face. *More screening, even in his choice of paintings!* I hadn't seen the painting on my previous visits. Had to be in a part of his house I hadn't seen. *His bedroom?*

His voice snapped me from my thoughts, 'Could we open our meeting with some grounding breaths?'

'Okay.'

I took several slow breaths in and out through my

nose at the now familiar rate he guided me through. *Four. Two. Five. Two.*

Too soon, he said, 'I can tell you've been practicing.'

He was right. I was now doing the breathing exercises almost every morning as soon as I woke up.

I smiled. 'Thanks.'

'You're welcome. How'd you go with the exercises?'

I lifted the book I'd placed on my desk beside me up to the webcam. 'I finished the book.'

'You read the sunflower book. I like that one.'

I couldn't stop myself from raising an eyebrow. 'You *do* read romance novels.'

He shrugged. 'Why not? They're good for reconnection exercises. What did the book teach you about men's interest?'

'It boils down to sunflowers.'

He smiled at my teasing. 'What did the sunflowers plot teach you?'

I thought back. 'After they'd had a fight, the hero brought the heroine a pot of mini sunflowers. He did this to apologise and show how well he knew her, by incorporating her favourite flower and her love for gardening into the apology gift. The potted sunflowers also acted as a symbol of his growth and him giving her his heart. She took them and planted them in her garden as a symbol of her own growth as well as accepting his heart and apology.'

'I don't think I could have said that better, but what does this tell you about signs a man is interested in you?'

'He'll buy you flowers.'

He grinned at my trite answer. 'And?'

'He'll pay attention to things that are important to you.'

'Yes. Anything else?'

'He'll work on his growth, not be afraid to share his heart with you, and he'll apologise when necessary.'

'Well done. Remember, all of those things go the other way, too.'

'What? Women have to buy men sunflowers as well? No fair. I want all the sunflowers.'

He laughed. 'You can have all the sunflowers.'

'Yay.'

'Now that's decided, would you be able to tell me three things you see that grab your attention?'

You. I drew in a sharp breath at the thought. What the hell? What was that? Emerson noticed. I knew because I saw the edges of his eyes crinkle with concern. *Please don't comment—*

'Everything all right?'

Crap.

'Yep. Everything's fine.'

Silence came from his side of the video link. I could see him puzzling out whether to push for more.

He must have decided to leave things because he said, 'In that case, are you ready to continue?'

Relieved, I answered, 'What did you want me to do again?'

'Name three things you see that grab your attention.'

Not *Emerson Novak* ... I put all my effort into disconnecting from that thought and focused instead on finding three things to name. Several colourful, comfy items caught my eye. 'The pillows.'

'What is it about them that caught your attention?'

I shrugged. 'I don't know.'

'Yes, you do. Can you look at them again? Tell me what you think about when you look at them. Doesn't have to be anything earth-shattering.'

I looked at the pillows, then said, 'They're soft, comfy, and have bright colours.'

'Great answer. Two more, please.'

I peered around the room, and felt a moment of surprise when I realised I was seeing it, truly seeing it, for the first time since I'd moved in. How had I not noticed the beautiful, despite being faded, gold filigree pattern set into the old cream wallpaper?

I smiled, then said, 'The wallpaper.'

'Why did it get your attention?'

'It's pretty.'

'How so?'

'It's faded, but if you look closely, you can see a pretty, gold filigree pattern set into it. Here, can you see it?' I turned the computer to angle the camera towards the paper.

'I see it. You're right, it's beautiful.'

I turned the computer camera back to me.

Emerson smiled, then said, 'One more.'

I glanced around and located something else I'd hardly paid attention to before but saw now in a new way. A gentle warmth settled in my chest as I stared at the item and said, 'Photo.'

Cara had secured the photo in the top right corner of the vanity table mirror.

'What do you like about it?'

'It's Cara and I on the day we graduated from uni. Cara brought her purple instant photo camera, and we took that selfie in our black caps and gowns. We were so happy. We went out afterwards to celebrate. It was so much fun.'

Had Cara put that photo there to remind me of that day? To comfort me when I felt sad? To show she would always be there for me? Probably for all those reasons, knowing her. I felt myself tear up. She was such a good friend. I was grateful to have her.

'Neoma?'

I blinked away the growing tears and nodded, 'I'm okay. Just thinking about how grateful I am to have Cara.'

'She's lucky to have you.'

I snorted. 'Other way around. I don't think I would have gotten through this time without her.'

'It helps to have a support person, doesn't it?'

'It really does.'

'I'm glad the photo reminds you of happy times.'

'Me, too. We have lots of good memories together.'

I had to remember that more often and not only lock onto that one awful night.

He smiled. 'Good memories are good.'

I laughed. 'Yes, they are.'

'I think it's safe to assume you're feeling good right now?'

'Yes, why?'

'Do you think you can locate the feeling for me?'

'What do you mean?'

'How do you *know* you feel good? Where do you *feel* it?'

I shrugged. 'In my head? My head is telling me it feels good.'

He shook his head. 'That's how you understand it, but the feeling is in your body, or your brain would have nothing to process. We feel things in our bodies all the time, but we aren't always conscious of it. You've performed body scans before, and the Vital Signs scan, what I would like you to do now is a modified body scan.'

'Modified how?'

'You'll be scanning for pleasant feelings, rather than tense feelings.'

'I don't know if I can do that.'

'Could you try?'

'Okay.'

'Fantastic. Take a slow breath, then close your eyes.'

I did.

His voice went down to the soothing tone I liked when he continued, 'I want you to think about the photo. Let the image and memories of that day come back to you.'

I let my mind drift backwards to the two of us walking and chatting with newly-graduated excitement along the university green …

Cara stopped me with a touch to my arm. When I turned to face her, she burst into laughter.

'What?'

She pointed to a building close to us and said, 'That's where we first met.'

I looked at the corner of the building and grinned. 'If that's what you want to call falling flat on our asses.'

That made her laugh again. 'Let's get a photo to remember our first and last day on this spot.'

I smiled and felt a warmth spread through my heart–

Emerson cut into my memory, saying, 'Start at your head. As you move your attention from your head to your toes, tell me if you feel something pleasant. Anything warm, tingly, expansive, or soft. No matter how subtle. It's all right if you don't feel anything––'

The sensations from the memory lingered inside me. I didn't need to start at my head. It was my turn to cut Emerson off.

I said, 'I can already feel where it is. My heart. I feel it in my heart.'

'Good job, Neoma. What do you feel?'

'Warmth.'

'Can you hold that feeling?'

'How?'

'Concentrate on your heart and the warmth you feel with that memory.'

I did that for about one second before I lost it.

My frustration must have shown because, before I could speak, he said, 'It's all right if you can't feel it anymore. That's perfectly normal if you've never done this exercise before. It will get easier with practice. Open your eyes for me, please.'

I opened them and jumped from shock when Emerson's face came into my line of vision. When he was concentrating, he looked startlingly handsome. Why was I only realising that now?

'Are you all right? What happened?'

Damn his observations.

'Nothing. Fly scared me.'

I lied. It was better than admitting I'd been startled by his beauty.

He accepted my explanation with a nod, then said, 'Those will be your tasks for this fortnight.'

'The modified body scans?'

'Yes, and the "interesting things" exercise. Write something in your journal at least three times for each exercise, if you can. More is better. Do you understand what you have to do for the "interesting things" exercise?'

'I think so. Note down three things I find interesting and why?'

'Yes. We do this exercise so you can recognise all the good things around you. What about the modified body scans? Do you remember how to do those?'

I nodded. 'Start from my head, work down to my toes, write down anything that feels good.'

'You're fast becoming the expert.'

I laughed at the faux horror on his face. 'Hardly.'

He grinned, then added, 'You can also write in your journal any time you notice yourself feeling good about something as well. When you get better at that, I want you to try to expand the length of time you feel good. Do you think you can do that?'

'Yes.'

'Fantastic. Again, the altered body scan exercise is designed to get you connected to your body and its positive sensations. Any questions so far?'

'Nope.'

'You've done really well today, Neoma.'

'Thank you.'

'You're welcome.'

Chapter Thirty Four

Emerson

A MOMENT of silence passed between us. Her eyes were glowing with what I guessed was a renewed confidence.

'You're doing so well, Neoma.' Most of my clients started out unable to feel their bodies fully. I had learned to expect it. Loss of connection to the body and its feelings was a common post-trauma symptom. A symptom often accompanied by harmful coping mechanisms, which helped survivors avoid a connection to the body and its troubling feelings. *Coping mechanisms such as alcohol and one-night stands?* I pushed away that snarky, unspoken remark and continued, 'I was wondering if you'd feel up to doing a more traditional body scan?'

'Now?'

'Yes.'

She shrugged. 'Why not?'

After getting her to draw in a slow breath and close her eyes, I said, 'I want you to focus your attention on your toes. Tell me how they feel.'

Toes were usually an innocuous body part, so they were an excellent place to start a body scan intended to align people to their bodily sensations, both good and bad.

'I'm not sure.'

'All right, let's start with temperature. Are they hot, cold, just right?'

'Just right, I guess.'

'Do they feel relaxed? Tense? Neither?'

'Neither.'

'Good. Now to your legs.'

She brought me back to reality when she said, 'They feel a little tight.'

Hmm. Her nervous system could be doing everything it could to 'keep her on guard'.

To test the theory, I said, 'I want you to tighten the muscles, then relax them. It might feel strange at first.'

I could see the concentration on her face, but eventually her features softened, and I could tell she was doing it.

She confirmed my conclusion by saying, 'Done.'

'Focus on your legs again. How do they feel?'

'Relaxed.'

'Good. Now ...' This part could be delicate. I drew in a breath, then said, 'Move your attention to your pelvic region.'

I saw her face scrunch up within seconds. Just as I'd suspected. She would be resistant to anything in her pelvic region. *She's definitely had sexual trauma.* I bit my lip and swallowed down the anger that threatened to rise with that thought. This was about Neoma, and helping her, not dealing with my feelings about it. I would need to move slower.

In order to prevent a triggered reaction in her, I opened my mouth to change her focus, but she interrupted, saying, 'It feels really tight. Really, *really,* tight.'

She squirmed in her seat.

I lowered my voice, keeping it soft, 'Move your attention from your pelvis now. Could you––'

'I can't.' Her breathing started rising.

'Focus on my voice. Slow your breathing for me.'

'I ...'

Her forehead crinkled then, and I knew I was losing her. The point of this exercise was to get Neoma in touch with her bodily sensations and feelings, not to freak her out. I had to find a way to calm her down. Fast.

'Neoma––'

'Why are you here?' She wasn't talking to me. Her voice sounded disconnected.

Oh-oh.

'Neoma––'

'You need to leave ... I said *leave.*'

She screamed before I could say anything. *No.* She was having a flashback. I'd pushed her too hard. *Idiot. My* chest felt like it would burst as I watched her breathing accelerate even more.

She pushed up from her chair and said, 'I can't breathe.'

I had to do something.

I couldn't leave her like that.

Especially when I was the one who'd caused it.

I jumped from my seat and said, 'Neoma, I'm coming.'

CHAPTER THIRTY FIVE

Emerson

I HAD ARRIVED at her house within ten minutes, but it felt longer. I didn't even bother to lock the car before I darted to her front door.

Banging on it, I yelled her name.

Nothing.

'Neoma!'

Still nothing. She had to be home. She would not have moved far in her dissociated state. I had to get inside to see if she was all right. Acting on instinct, I barged at the door with my shoulder. It didn't budge. I didn't let that stop me. Using every ounce of strength I could pull up, I rushed at the door again. When that didn't work, I started kicking. And punching. I barged, punched, and kicked the door until I heard a crack. That crack was the sweetest sound I had heard in years. I kicked at the faint line in the door that appeared. *Crack.* A bigger crack appeared. I attacked that crack until I could push my way through.

Once inside the house, I started calling her name again. Still nothing. I bolted up the hallway and opened the door to the first room I saw. A bedroom, but not hers. The wallpaper was not cream. No gold filigree. I moved to the next door. A bathroom.

Frowning, I called her name again, 'Neoma?'

Nothing. *Where are you?* Three more doors lined the hallway. Which was it? Each second I lost could make a difference. *Which one?* An answer came. *The one at the end.* That one would be hers because it was furthest from the front door. It gave her space from potential intruders and more time to escape. I rushed forward and opened the door. A quick scan of the room showed Neoma, bundled in the corner in a foetal position. Her eyes were closed as she shivered and rocked herself in a gentle motion. *Movement is good.* I ran to her side and knelt down. She whimpered and cowered away from me. I could see tears had stained her cheeks.

Without touching her––that could trigger her further––I whispered, 'Neoma, it's me. It's Emerson.'

She turned her head and opened her eyes. I saw the faintest beam of recognition in them.

I repeated, 'It's Emerson. You're safe.'

Her whimpers eased.

I stared deep into her eyes and added, 'I won't hurt you. You know that, right?'

She looked me up and down, as if she was trying to pick who I was, then responded with a subtle nod. *Good.* That meant she was coming back to the present.

'I'm going to sit with you, all right?'

She nodded. Again, it was subtle, but it was there. I sat down in front of her and tried to lock her gaze, but her eyes darted everywhere. *Looking for a way to escape.* She was stuck on that border between the past and present. She'd depersonalised or dissociated, maybe both, because of the flashback. Post-traumatic episodes varied in length, so it was difficult to say how long this one would last. She'd shown signs of coming out of it already: the small nods. I knew I could bring her through with emotional support to connect her to her body and pull her to the present.

In a soft, low tone, I said, 'I'm with you and you're safe. Can you look around the room and tell me something you see that you like?'

I watched her gaze shift upwards. The haziness in her stare showed she was still not present.

Her croaky voice said, 'Emerson.'

I smiled. Her logical brain was coming online. 'Yes, Neoma. It's Emerson. I'm here.'

She responded with a faint smile. *Good sign.* Then, she did something I was unprepared for. She put her head on my shoulder. *Wow.* That showed her trust in me. Happiness filled my chest. Her body relaxed against mine. An instant later, Neoma looked up at me. I could see the former haziness clearing from her eyes. Her expression, so vulnerable, so trusting, made my insides twist in a strange way. What did it mean? I ignored that question and focused on the most important point: this had been my fault. If I hadn't been so focused on myself, this wouldn't have happened. I'd let Neoma down.

She spoke, low and uncertain, 'Emerson?'

'Yes, it's me.'

She pulled back to get a better look at my face. Her features turned serious as she asked, 'What happened? Why are you here? Why ...' She glanced down, then back up and continued, 'Why are we sitting so close?'

I blurted out, 'I'm so sorry. I should have been here. No, I should have had you in my office, so you didn't have to go through that flashback alone.'

'I had a flashback?'

'What in the actual fuck happened here?'

We both turned our heads. Cara stood on the threshold of Neoma's bedroom looking down at us with a mixture of confusion, protective instinct, and anger on her face. Neoma went to stand up but wobbled. Cara rushed forward and grabbed Neoma before I could, then threw me a wary glance.

I rose as Cara led Neoma to the bed and helped her lay down. Once settled, Cara looked at Neoma and asked, 'What happened?'

'I'm not really sure ...' Neoma glanced my way, which made Cara do the same.

I opened my mouth to explain, then realised Neoma might want the details kept private. Even though they were best friends, and Cara had been instrumental in getting Neoma to see me, it didn't give Cara the right to Neoma's personal business. I didn't even know if this was Neoma's first dissociative episode. Neoma might not want others to know either way.

'I think Neoma and I should have a private talk about that first.'

Cara scoffed. 'You think I'm going to leave you alone with my best friend after what I've walked in on? Hell no, mister. The door is busted, Neo is confused, and nobody is giving me answers.' Before I could respond, she barrelled forward until we were face-to-face. With visibly growing anger and protection instinct, she added, 'You might be some fancy-smancy therapist, but I will not let you or any other man take––'

Neoma cut in, 'Emerson wasn't taking advantage of me. He was helping me. I ... dissociated.'

She's used the word. She could name and, in doing so, accept the effects of trauma on herself.

Cara frowned at me, obviously still unsure of my role in everything, then stepped towards her friend's bedside. 'That's why you don't remember?'

Cara had apparently witnessed Neoma's episodes before and understood at a basic level what dissociation involved.

Neoma nodded.

'Then, can you please tell him to explain it?' She emphasised the word 'him' in a still-accusing way.

Neoma glanced up at me but avoided making eye contact when she said, 'It's okay. You can tell her.'

With permission granted, Cara bombarded me with questions, 'Why are you here? I thought this was going to be an online session? And what happened to the front door?'

'We *were* having an online session. During one of the exercises, I noticed Neoma starting to dissociate, so I drove over so she wouldn't have to go through it alone. When she didn't answer the door, I got worried and––'

Cara interrupted, finishing my sentence, 'Kicked the door in?'

'Yes.'

Cara sighed, seeming to relax now that she had an explanation. Turning to Neoma, she studied her friend's face, then said, 'You still look pale. Do you want me to make you some tea?'

'That would be nice.'

'I should probably get someone to fix that door, too.'

'I damaged it, so I'll pay for it.'

Cara waved my offer away. 'Not necessary. I know someone who can do it.'

'Are you sure?'

'Yes. By the way, sorry I was harsh, but not sorry, because I was worried.'

'Totally understandable.'

'Thank you for coming.'

'It was the least I could do.'

Cara snorted, then looked at Neoma. 'I doubt any of Neo's other counsellors would have done this.'

'It wasn't a problem.'

Cara went to walk out of the bedroom but stopped to say to me, 'Would you like a tea, too?'

'No, I have to get back, but thank you for the offer.'

If I didn't have another meeting scheduled, I might have taken Cara up on the tea to monitor Neoma. The aftereffects of a dissociative episode could be unpleasant: fatigue, headaches, restlessness, inability to concentrate, negative thoughts, lack of motivation, upset stomach. My own stomach churned with worry.

Once we were alone, I took a free spot at the end of the bed and said, 'How are you feeling?'

'Tired.'

'Try to get some sleep after I leave.'

'I will.'

'This has happened before.' I didn't make it a question.

She nodded. 'It hasn't happened in weeks, so why now? I thought I was doing so well.' She sighed, and I could hear the weariness in it.

'You *are* doing well. Brilliant, in fact.'

'Then, why did this happen?' She looked at me with imploring eyes. I realised I'd asked Sil the same question.

I gave Neoma an answer Sil had given me once, 'Trauma recovery isn't a staircase. You don't go up in a straight line. It's more like an ascending spiral. You might go around in circles sometimes, but you're still making progress.'

'It doesn't feel like that. It feels like I've fallen off the staircase.'

'You and I both know that's the aftereffects of the dissociation talking. Once you have a sleep, you'll feel better.'

'Yeah.'

When she raised a hand to her head, I asked, 'Do you have a headache?'

She lowered her hand. 'A little.'

'The tea and sleep should help. Why don't you get under the covers?'

'What about the tea?'

'I'm sure Cara will bring it up. In the meantime, you can get comfortable and rest.' I rose and pulled the blankets down on the side she wasn't occupying. 'Here. Hop in.'

She faltered for a second, then came around me and slipped under the covers. I placed the blanket up over her. 'Get some sleep. I'll call tomorrow morning to check in on you.'

Her eyes were already closed and her voice had drifted off.

I waited a moment, watching her slow, even breaths. She was asleep. I watched her a moment, to make sure her breaths were easy and relaxed. A piece of her fringe flicked into her eyelashes. I wanted to reach down and push the hair aside, but I didn't want to do anything that might retrigger her. Instead, I turned around. Cara was standing in the doorway with a cup and saucer. She nodded for me to come out.

When I did, she said in a whisper, 'My friend, Oliver, and Neoma's friend, Raj, are coming over in an hour to fix the door.'

When I drove off minutes later, I realised I was frowning. Why? Was I still upset over Neoma's dissociative episode? Or was it something else? For some reason, one word hummed through my head.

Raj.

CHAPTER THIRTY SIX

Neoma

EMERSON STARED DOWN AT ME, concern beaming from his eyes. A moment later, he reached down and brushed a strand of hair from my face. His fingers felt warm and soft. I wanted them to stay there, but they moved away, leaving my heart thumping––

I woke with a start at the sound of my phone ringing. I groaned and reached towards my bedside table to shut it off. A yawn made me open my eyes in time to see Emerson's name flashing on the screen. *Emerson ...*

I bolted upright. Had I just had a dream about him? *Gods, no.* And now he was calling. Why? *I'll call tomorrow morning to check in on you.* Had that been part of my dream, or had he actually said that? The phone kept ringing in my hand. Trying to clear the sleep from my throat, I answered.

'Oh, no. Did I wake you?'

'It's okay. I need to be getting up for work, anyway.'

'I can write you a medical certificate if you need it?'

'Appreciated, but I feel fine.'

'Are you sure?'

'Yes, I even used the *feel* word.' He chuckled, but I intuited no genuine humour behind it. I could tell he was still concerned about me. To reassure him, I said, 'Honestly, Emerson, having something to do other than look at the bedroom walls will be good for me. It's only four hours. I can handle it.'

'I have no doubt that you can.'

'Thank you.'

'You're welcome. Did you get much sleep?'

'More than I usually get after an episode.'

'Glad to hear it ... Did Raj come to fix the door?'

'I've only just woken up, so I have no idea what's been going on.'

'Oh, right. Of course. I should let you get ready for work, then.'

'Thanks for checking in.'

'No problem. I'm happy you're doing well.'

'Me, too.'

'Is it all right if I text you later about our next meeting date?'

'Yes.'

We said our goodbyes, then I switched off the alarm I'd set on my phone and got up to take a shower. I didn't want to be late to work when I hadn't been back for long and was only working part-time hours. They'd never let me back full-time if I kept stuffing up and causing unnecessary problems. The fact they'd been so understanding already was amazing.

I grabbed my things for the shower and made my way to the bathroom. Once I'd finished, I could make Cara breakfast. She might die from the shock. I chuckled to myself as I turned on the water. The sight of water dropping to the floor pulled a memory forward. Of the day Emerson and I had first met. When he'd picked up my dropped water bottles. Now I was remembering ... his arms had looked flipping sexy when he'd heaved the bottles up from the ground. I groaned at the memory. What was going on? First, I'd dreamed about him, now I was having ... thoughts ... about him. *Ack.* I was being stupid. Maybe I should make this a cold shower to freeze images of Emerson from my mind?

CHAPTER THIRTY SEVEN

Emerson

NEOMA HAD ASSURED me she was fine. She'd sounded fine. *Everything's fine.* I inhaled to calm the worry I'd been feeling all morning, then searched through my calendar for a space to fit Neoma in. There was an appointment free next week and one in a fortnight. With everything that had happened, a closer date was better. I shot her a text message with the appointment details.

Then, I tried to focus on the meeting I was supposed to be having with Jack in five minutes. Most of our meetings and phone calls over the past eighteen months had been rehashed versions of our first formal meeting--'I have an interview/podcast/vlog spot for you. Still working on that book deal and retreats.' Others might have suspected he was playing me. Aside from instinct telling me that wasn't the case, the facts proved that assumption wrong. Jack *did* get me regular spots, the web series had performed well, and he was working for a pittance until I signed the book contract he'd promised me in our first meeting. With the thought, a knock on the front door filtered through to my office. I let Jack in and showed him to my desk.

Before I could speak, he said, 'Do you want the good news or the excellent news first?'

'The excellent news.'

'You have a book deal.'

'What?'

Had I heard right?

He grinned, then placed several sheets of paper on my desk. 'You have a year from the date of signing to give them a manuscript.'

'A year!'

Jack waved his hands in a calming action. 'Don't worry. I already have an experienced ghost writer signed to help you out. What day next week do you have available to meet with her?'

Ghost writer. Next week. Book deal. My brain looped those words, trying to put them together in a way that made sense.

'Wait ... this is really happening?'

Jack smiled. 'Yes, Emerson. It's really happening.'

'Wow. I'm in shock.'

'I told you this was going to happen, didn't I?'

'You did, but ...'

'You thought I was all hot air?'

I shook my head. 'It's not that. I don't know. It's a lot to process.'

'You *do* want this still, don't you?'

Did I? It would let me reach so many people. It could show the world that unorthodox therapy had its place in mental health. It would give therapists and clients more options. I wanted to help people, right? This was my chance to do that on an international scale.

'Yes.'

'Beautiful. When are you free for lunch?'

I flicked through the calendar on my phone and said, 'Wednesday.'

'I'll set up a lunch date for the two of you to meet and discuss your vision for the book.'

'What *is* my vision for the book?'

'You'll have until Wednesday to figure that out. Trust yourself, I'm sure you'll come up with something. If not, that's what Rose is for.'

'Rose is the ghost writer?'

'Correct. I'll text you the details once she's confirmed her availability.' I nodded as he added, 'Do you want to hear the good news now?'

'Do I need to sit down first?'

'Couldn't hurt.'

Once I was seated, Jack said, 'You've also been offered a series of overseas group retreats, starting in six months.' He placed another stack of papers beside the first. 'And, you'll have an all-expenses paid book tour two months before the book releases. Plus, I have at least fifteen interviews, podcasts, and television shows lined up for you starting next year. You're going to be a busy man.'

Next year. That gave me about two months before my life changed forever. Was I ready for this?

Jack spoke again, 'I've hired an assistant to help manage your socials, marketing, promotions, and anything else you'll need. His name is Seunie. Should you decide to sign the contracts, he'll also start next week.'

'Is that necessary?'

He scoffed. 'Have you been awake the past decade?'

'I'm taking that as a "yes".'

'You'd be right.'

'How will I pay for all this?'

'So glad you asked. Firstly, you'll be able to afford it.' He lifted a hand to silence me when I opened my mouth to object, 'Wait until you see the insane amount you have been offered for the book and retreats. Seunie wants you to start a more regular video series as well, and I'm sure we can get you on a speaking tour at some stage. Both of those will add to your bank balance. After you go through all the paperwork, if you have questions, let me know.'

'I already have a thousand questions.'

'Try to narrow it down before you call me.'

'Will do.'

Jack grinned. 'Didn't I say you were going to be a star, Trauma Guru?'

'You did.'

A lump formed in my throat. I would have to lower my case load and not take on any new clients. I'd have to set aside time to write the book and organise retreat schedules. There was so much to do and the time frame felt like it was closing in on me. Having an assistant and ghost writer was looking better by the second.

Jack frowned. 'Why aren't you excited?'

'I am. I'm trying to work out everything in my head. This is all happening so fast.'

'Fast? This has been eighteen months in the making, my friend.'

'I know ... and I am grateful. It's a lot to process.'

Jack nodded. 'I understand. But this is going to help a lot of people. *You* are going to help a lot of people. That's what you want, isn't it?'

'It is.'

'Beautiful. Call me once you've had your lawyer read over everything.'

I nodded. Thank goodness a lawyer was one thing I *did* have sorted out. I'd hired Anna-Lee when Jack had offered to represent me. Once Jack had gone, I picked up the book contract. When I saw the number making up the publisher's payment offer on the page, I was grateful to be sitting down. I had to recount the zeroes to make sure I was reading right. Jack hadn't been kidding when he'd said I could afford an assistant and ghost writer. And that was only the book contract. I picked up the retreats contract. If eyeballs could pop out, mine would have. People could actually be paid this much to do these things? *I w*as going to be paid this much? My mind whirred with the possibilities that many zeroes afforded me. I could expand my private practice, hold regular group therapy sessions, rent out a proper building instead of using my home. My chest was racing. I felt myself smile ... then frowned when another consequence of all this hit me. I would be hosting retreats and tours all over the place. I wouldn't be able to see the people I loved for ... I didn't even know how long. What about my current clients?

What about Neoma?

My phone pinged, pulling me from the answer. Funnily enough, the name on the screen matched the name that had been in my mind. I read her text. *Thursday morning next week works for me.* I shot back a brief message. *See you then.* After pressing 'send,' I was about to place my phone down, when my hand stopped. An impulse went through me and made my fingers type another message. *Hope you are having a good day.* I'd sent it before I could double-think the decision. A second later, my phone beeped with a reply. *I'm doing great. Stop worrying about me and go do something productive.* I smiled, hearing the teasing tone in her voice, as if she'd said it to me herself. I sent back: *Like what?* Her answer: *Get yourself an apple crumble muffin ... and bring me one while you're at it.* I laughed. Then, realised my fingers had typed and sent something else. *Deal. What's the address of your work?*

I gasped. What. Had. I. Done? A stretch of silence passed between us that seemed to drag on forever. Had I gone too far? Was it too unprofessional? The returned message beep cut off my thoughts. I opened the message with half-closed eyes. What if she was telling me to go to hell? I peered down and sighed in relief. An address. Too late to back out now. My fingers agreed, sending my response: *Be there soon.*

Chapter Thirty Eight

Neoma

What have I done? Emerson was on his way. Was that okay? A soft knock on my office door made me jump. I sucked in a breath. Had Emerson arrived already? *No.* He would have to have been outside the building to get to my office so fast. Another knock filtered towards me and I realised my startled reaction had been from the unexpectedness of the knock, rather than it reminding me of my past. Maybe Emerson was right, and I was making progress 'in a spiral'?

I couldn't help smiling before I called out, 'Come in.'

My boss walked in. Sabrina noticed my smile, and the phone in my hand. She frowned. 'Am I interrupting?'

'Not at all.'

Sabrina closed the door behind her. 'There's something I wanted to talk to you about.'

Oh-oh. The serious look on her face said this would not be good. Was she firing me? Oh, no. Why? Was this about the 'incident?'

Confused, I said, 'I thought I was doing well?'

'You are. It's not about that.'

I tried to keep my relief under control when I asked, 'What's it about?'

'Do you want to sit?'

'Depends on what you have to say.'

She shot me a look, so I returned to the seat behind my desk. She sat on one of the chairs in front of my desk.

Then, she charged right in, saying, 'I'm assuming you've noticed Peter isn't around.'

'I hadn't thought about it, but ... yes, now that you've mentioned it.'

'I wanted you to know that we fired him.'

'Okay.' What did that have to do with me?

Sabrina gave me another confused look before adding, 'Because of what he did to you.'

What he did to me? What was she talking about? The second I thought it, memories washed over me. That sleazy Peter from Accounting had sexually harassed me soon after the other incident on my birthday. He'd stood close to me when I was at the printer. That had triggered me. I'd told him, more politely than he'd deserved, to give me some space. Instead, he'd moved closer, touched my arm, and said something along the lines of, 'I'm just trying to be friendly.' Yeah, that old clichéd chestnut. Then, he'd moved closer, touched my face ... and I'd gone as crazy as a virus-infected bat at him. I think I scratched his face. I hope I did. I hope it left scars. Physical *and* emotional. *Asshole.*

I nodded, not sure what she wanted me to say.

Sabrina continued, 'Apparently, you weren't the first. A bunch of women came forward after you went on stress leave.'

Stress leave. They put me on forced *stress leave.* All this time, I'd assumed I was on forced probationary leave. I exhaled with relief. Both at remembering what had happened that day and from the knowledge that I wasn't the cause of it. I had no reason to feel embarrassed or ashamed. *You have no reason to feel that way about the incident on your birthday, either.*

Sabrina spoke, cutting off any response I could have made to the thought, 'I hope that makes you feel safer and more comfortable here. I want you to know we don't endorse that behaviour.'

'Thank you, Sabrina.'

She nodded, then left me alone. In the silence of my office, I realised I was smiling. For the first time in months, I'd had flashbacks and not freaked out. Add that to my not being triggered by the knock on my door, and I felt amazing. Emerson's voice came to me then. *How do you* know *you feel amazing?* I closed my eyes and started a modified body scan, running from the top of my head, searching for feelings in my body that confirmed the feeling. I found it when I reached my heart area. It felt wide, free, and open. I laughed. All of this was because of Emerson. *No, Neo,* you *did this.* Emerson had pointed the way, but I'd walked the path. It'd been a long time since I'd felt so good. Once Emerson arrived, I would need to remember to thank him.

CHAPTER THIRTY NINE

Emerson

BY THE TIME we'd sat down at the park benches, in a shady area due to the full sun, the initial awkwardness of the situation dissolved with our friendly chatter. I had to admit, Neoma looked as 'fine' as she'd claimed. This was the first time I'd seen her with her hair brushed and down with a full face of makeup. Both enhanced her natural beauty. I'd noticed men snatching glances at her as we walked. It had bothered me, on her behalf, of course.

Neoma swallowed her first bite of muffin, then said, 'Mmm. This is so good it's going in my journal later.'

The near-orgasmic look on her face sent a flush of warmth right down where it was inappropriate to be feeling such things right now.

I pushed away the reaction and said, 'Don't tell Frank I bought it somewhere else.'

'Your secret is safe with me.'

Her phone pinged with a message. I peered over in time to see her frowning at it.

'What's wrong?'

She looked at me. 'My mother.'

'Your tone hints at issues with her.'

'Yes.'

'Do you want to talk about it?'

She hesitated, then glanced around us in a gesture that said she was making sure nobody was listening, then said, 'After the attack, she kept barraging me with unhelpful questions and comments.'

'Parents can make mental health issues worse.'

I let the silence between us grow as I took a bite from my muffin, so Neoma could decide if she wanted to share anything more with me without feeling pressured.

She took a couple of nibbles from her muffin, then added, 'I haven't spoken to her in a couple of months.'

'Because of the comments?'

I took another bite from my muffin, waiting for her answer.

She sighed with a nod. 'Even when I asked mum to stop, she didn't. She would say things like "You stupid girl" and "Why would you do such a stupid thing."' She scoffed. 'I *know* I was stupid. I didn't need her to keep pointing it out.'

'You weren't stupid, Neoma.'

'You don't know everything that happened.'

'I know enough.'

'You might change your mind once you know the full story.'

'You *weren't* to blame for what happened. There's nothing you could tell me that will change my mind about that.'

'Nothing?' She straightened, as though she took that word as a challenge.

I nodded, then emphasised the word back at her, 'Nothing.'

She inhaled, hesitated, then said, 'The attack happened on my birthday.'

'Oh, Neoma.' My heart felt like it had been stabbed with a thousand swords.

She looked down. 'I'd booked an event room at a club. A few of my friends came. Cara couldn't come because she was working, but we'd arranged for her to meet up at my apartment afterwards.'

She peeked up, uncertainty in her eyes. I gave an encouraging nod.

'Sometime during the night, some guys from outside started sending in free drinks "to celebrate the birthday girl". I didn't see the harm in accepting. I thought they were being nice.'

Her lip trembled. The urge to touch her hand, to comfort her, came. I knew it would be crossing a professional line if I gave in, so I forced myself to remain still as I said, 'They weren't being nice, were they?'

She shook her head, then stared deep into my eyes. I could see moisture forming in her eyes and knew my own weren't far off.

'When I came out, I was a little tipsy, not drunk, but not fully sober either.'

I nodded. *Was this the reason she'd given up drinking?*

'A couple of the guys came up and introduced themselves. One started getting too friendly, so I told him to get lost. He called me a few choice names, so I mouthed off again. Some bouncers intervened, and I went outside to wait for the ride I'd ordered.'

She swallowed hard, then looked down. Tears had filled her eyes and one escaped down her cheek. She wiped it away, sniffling.

I said in a low voice, 'It's all right. I'm here.'

She looked over at me. 'I didn't know some of them had followed me back to my apartment. I didn't know until they knocked on my door. I thought it was Cara.' She shook her head. 'I should have checked.'

I shook my head. 'You weren't to know. Most people wouldn't have checked, Neoma.'

'I suppose so.' After a moment, she continued, 'I opened the door, and they barged in. I'm still fuzzy on the specifics, but my clothes got ripped, I had bruises on my arms and face, and I remember ...'

She broke into a sob.

My chest felt heavy and hard––both upset and angry for her. An almost desperate need to comfort her by placing an arm around her swirled through me. Even though it was hard, I still resisted. She might get triggered by my touch.

Wanting to do something, I said, 'I'm sorry that happened.'

She covered her face with her palms.

Between muffled sobs, I heard her say, 'Their hands. I remember their hands. They were *everywhere.*'

I pressed my lips together, then exhaled to simultaneously control my anger and the renewed urge to rub comforting circles over her back.

I whispered, 'I'm so sorry.'

In a flicker of insight, I realised I was apologising for the trauma she had experienced as well as to myself for feeling as bound by circumstances now as I had during my own trauma experience. To counteract that thought, I visualised rubbing comforting circles over her back. *Movement is good.*

CHAPTER FORTY

Neoma

EMERSON ALWAYS MANAGED to make me feel calm. The softness in his voice echoed through my mind. And, even though I knew it was my imagination, it felt like his hand was rubbing circles over my back. My tears soon dried up.

Wiping the tears from my eyes, I looked at him and said, 'Thanks for listening.'

'Any time.'

'And thanks for the muffin.'

'You're welcome.'

'And, for the sessions. They've really helped.'

He smiled, big and genuine. 'I'm so happy for you, Neoma.'

'It's all thanks to you.'

He shook his head. 'You did the hard work. My techniques mean nothing without the person practicing them.'

'You don't give yourself enough credit.'

'Neither do you.'

'We're both as bad as each other.'

He laughed. 'Looks like it.'

I smiled, and an alarm on my phone went off. I pulled the phone from my pocket and stopped switched the alarm off.

Looking at Emerson, I said, 'My break's over.'

'Let's head back.'

We wrapped up our half-eaten muffins and walked in the direction of the publishing house. Emerson had insisted on chaperoning me back to my office. As we stepped from the elevator, Sabrina saw us.

She stopped, and pointed at Emerson, 'I know you.'

'I don't think so.'

'Yes, yes, I do. You're Emerson Novak.'

I gave him a playful look. 'I didn't know you're famous.'

He grinned as Sabrina said, 'He's going to be bigger than any other TV psychologist soon.'

I glanced at him, then at Sabrina, curiosity firing in my belly. 'Why?'

'He's just signed a contract with us ... at least, I hope you will soon, Mister Novak.'

I looked at Emerson, who was avoiding my gaze. *He's got a contract with us?* He hadn't said anything.

He stammered, 'I'll let you know.'

Sabrina smiled. 'Your book will help millions of people.'

'Thank you.'

Something seemed to occur to her then. She looked at both of us, and said, 'You two know each other?'

I cut in, 'We're recently acquainted.'

'Perfect. You can request Neoma to be your editor if you sign with us.'

He *did glance* at me then. 'I'll keep that in mind.'

'By the way, my name is Sabrina Guttenberg. Please call me if you have any questions.'

'I will.'

'It was a pleasure to meet you in person.'

She held out her hand and Emerson shook it. Then, she left us alone.

I faced him. 'Congratulations, Emerson. I'm thrilled for you.'

Getting a publishing contract was one of the most difficult things to achieve. He'd done well.

In a lowered tone, he said, 'I was going to tell you, I swear. I only received the contract five minutes before I came here. I didn't even have the chance to see which publishing company it was.'

'Relax, Emerson. I'm not upset you didn't tell me. This is a lot to wrap your head around.'

'It is. My manager, Jack, couldn't understand why I was in shock before.'

I smiled. 'You should celebrate.'

'I haven't signed the contract yet.'

'You will.'

'You seem confident.'

'I am. This is the best publishing company in the country.'

'You work here, you have to say that.'

'No, I don't. Somebody taught me it's okay for me to speak the truth.'

He smiled. 'Sounds like a smart guy.'

'He is, which is why I know he'll go back and sign that contract.'

He laughed. 'All right, because you insist.'

'Really? All I have to do is ask and you'll do my bidding? This could get interesting.' I steepled my hands in a mock-evil gesture.

'I have no doubt.'

I smiled as the air between us grew warm ... and electric. *Oh, no.* What was happening? The truth pounded through my brain. I'd told Emerson everything was fine. But it wasn't. It was far from fine. Because I was in trouble. Terrible, terrible trouble. Because ...

I'd developed *feelings* for Emerson Novak.

Feelings beyond a crush.

Ah!

This couldn't happen. It was inappropriate. Wasn't it? I shouldn't feel like this about my trauma recovery facilitator. What the heck was I going to do? I'd told him I would come to the next session, but how could I? It would be humiliating. How could I hide how I felt? At the same time, how could I cancel? If I did, he would ask why. *Which brings me back to cancelling because I'd feel humiliated.* What should I do? *Get away from him so you can think.*

Obeying the unspoken command, I said, 'I have to go.'

We said our goodbyes, and I forced myself to march straight to my office without looking back.

At my desk a short time later, I distracted myself from making a final decision by reading over my mother's text message: *Hi, darling. I know you said not to call, and I have tried to respect that. I've only been calling because I want to apologise. I know now what I did was wrong. I'm so sorry. Please call me back. I love you, Mum xo*

It sounded genuine. What if it wasn't? The healing and growth I'd undergone in the past months was undeniable. Was I strong enough not to have a setback if I spoke to her only to discover she hadn't meant it? I could always ask Cara to be there with me when I spoke to my mother? I would talk to her tonight, then go from there. Putting my phone back into my bag, I tried to focus on my work tasks. *Tried.*

Thoughts of Emerson zipped in and out of my brain for the rest of my time in the office. Which only made the situation more complicated. What was I supposed to do? Continuing ignoring it or confront it? Intuition told me I we would be forced to confront it, eventually. Would it end well? Part of me wanted the answer, another part wanted to pretend nothing was happening. Never was I more thankful to be on part-time hours than when my alarm reminded me it was time to pack up and leave. I'd been careful to set alarms to keep me on track and stop myself from slipping into old workaholic patterns. That was not going to happen today. I had far too much to talk about with Cara. First, whether I should call my mother. *Then, what to do about Emerson Novak.*

Chapter Forty One

Neoma

CARA DIDN'T HAVE time to breathe before I blurted everything out to her. She'd agreed to be with me when and if I eventually contacted my mother. As for the Emerson situation ...

She paused a moment, then said, 'I've been tossing up whether to tell you or not.'

'Tell me what?'

'Emerson likes you. In fact, I think he's pretty close to being in love with you.'

'What? No.'

'Yes, Neo. The guy *broke down our front door* for you.'

'He was just doing his job.'

'The only men who break down doors as part of their jobs are firemen and policemen. Is Emerson either of those?'

'No.'

'Point proven. Besides that, I've suspected his attraction for you since that day at *Frank's*. But I didn't realise his feelings had changed into something more serious until I saw the way he looked at you while you slept after your dissociative episode.'

I gulped. *How much of my dream had been real?*

'Why didn't you tell me?'

'He was helping you, and I wasn't sure how you felt about him. I wasn't going to get in the way if there was nothing to worry about. When you didn't say "no" to the dates with Raj, I assumed it was a one-sided thing on his end.'

'I called things off with Raj.'

'I know, but that didn't mean you felt anything for Emerson. So I kept my mouth shut.'

I groaned. 'What am I supposed to do now?'

'I wish I had an easy answer for you, Neo. Unfortunately, I think that's something you and Emerson will need to figure out for yourselves. Whatever you do decide, you know I'll be here, right?'

'I know. Thanks, Cara.'

She came in for a hug, so I wrapped my arms around her.

When she pulled away, she said, 'How about I make us some tea, then we can talk some more about the easier topic, your mother.'

I pulled a face, which made Cara laugh. 'I'm taking that as a "yes".'

She pranced off and left me to my thoughts. Which was not a good thing. The possibility that Emerson had feelings for me both thrilled and scared me. Would he have professional restrictions around a therapist-client romantic relationship?

I yelled out in frustration, 'Ack!'

From the kitchen, Cara called out, 'You okay, sweetie?'

'No.'

'Don't worry, we'll sort this out.'

I crossed my fingers. *Please, let that be true.*

Chapter Forty Two

Emerson

I'D SIGNED the contract the instant I'd returned from Neoma's office, but it had taken my lawyer until Wednesday to get back to me.

She said, 'I'm not happy you signed it before sending it to me.'

'But?'

'It's an excellent contract and my advice would have been to sign it. You have good instincts, Emerson. That's what makes you such a good therapist.'

It's what helped you get everyone out that day, too.

I shut down that thought, by saying, 'Thank you.'

'I'll look over the retreats contract and get back to you.'

I hadn't signed that one, which should make her

happy. We said our goodbyes, and I was left in the silence, with my thoughts. My life was going forward. This would be a new chapter. *Isn't it time you head into the future by resolving the past?* As much as my brain could be annoying, it had a point this time. I had told Sil I would call him about seeing a therapist. I picked up my phone and dialled. Half an hour later, I had two names and numbers. An hour later, I had my first therapy session––the psychologist had called it a session, so I would, too–– booked. Feeling more relaxed about that than I would have been six months ago, I wasn't prepared when an alert on my phone went off. I picked it up and saw a note: *meeting with Ghost Writer.*

'Shoot.'

I'd forgotten. Between Anna-Lee, Sil, and the new therapist, my focus had been pre-occupied. As exhausted as I was feeling, I couldn't cancel. This was also an important step towards my future. Resigned, I rose and went to the kitchenette in my home office to make myself a strong cup of coffee. Even though we'd arranged to meet at some type of posh French-themed patisserie, and I would, no doubt, end up getting another coffee there, I'd need caffeine rushing deep in my veins to get through the meeting. It had better be worth it. I finished with the coffee and returned to my desk. Taking a sip, I flipped my phone calendar to the next day. My gaze landed on one name. *Neoma.* I smiled. Since her episode, we'd decided on a face-to-face meeting this time around. This way, I could keep a closer eye on her and check for micro-signs of agitation. *Might even keep the screen away this time.* I felt my eyebrows lift in surprise at that thought. What the hell? I'd never wanted to do a meeting minus the screens before. What would Sil think about that? Or, my new therapist? What did *I* think about it?

Before taking another much-needed sip of coffee, I muttered under my breath, 'Wish I knew.'

Chapter Forty Three

Neoma

This was my first day off, and I'd been looking forward to a relaxing day. Except ... Cara sneezed. I looked to where she'd laid herself under a blanket on the couch. Her puffy, runny eyes and red nose evidenced the cold she'd developed overnight.

My best friend blew her nose then grumbled, 'I feel like a scone.'

'I can go to *Frank's* if you like?'

'You would?'

'Anything for my best friend.'

She smiled. 'You're the best, Neo.'

'Yeah, but don't tell me too often or it'll go to my head.'

'Not likely.'

I laughed. 'See you soon.'

'Hey, can you not tell Oliver I'm sick? He'll worry too much.'

'No probs.'

I grabbed Cara's keys from the kitchen counter, then drove to *Frank's*. For the first time ever, there were no car parks. *Busy for a Wednesday.* But, I wasn't going back empty-handed. I drove to Cara's second favourite treats place: a chic French patisserie called something in French I could never remember, let alone pronounce. This time, I scored a spot right out the front. *It's fate.*

Smiling to myself, I exited the car, opened the door of the patisserie, and stepped inside. Once I'd ordered at the front counter, I peered around. Towards the back of the restaurant section, I saw someone's side profile that made me pause. *Is that Emerson?* I opened my mouth to call out to him when I saw someone with him. A woman I didn't know. Who was she? A client? *Not the way they're huddled together like that.* That didn't necessarily mean anything. *We* got pretty close to each other at my work. The woman leaned towards Emerson. He laughed at something she said. A ball squeezed in my stomach. I was jealous. That was definitely *not* an appropriate emotion for my therapist. I'd been struggling over whether to cancel our session together or not. This reaction told me what I had to do. I couldn't see him again.

I was thankful when the counter assistant took that moment to give me the bag containing my order, because I could avoid looking at Emerson and leave with Cara's treat. By the time I'd driven into her driveway, I'd been able to slow-breathe my way to a shaky sense of calm. I shut down the car's engine and placed my head on the steering wheel. Emerson was dating, and it had made me upset and jealous to see it. I knew I had to cancel our session. Yet ... would I be okay without him? Was I ready to go out on my own? Was I strong enough?

CHAPTER FORTY FOUR

Emerson

I RE-READ Neoma's text message and felt myself frown. There was something off about it. Why would Neoma say she didn't need any more meetings out of the blue like this? Why do it via text message, instead of face-to-face or a phone call? With no proper explanation? Something was wrong. The instant my lunch meeting finished, I drove to her place. I expected Cara to answer the door, but it was Neoma. A look of surprise crossed her face before she crossed her arms. *Something's off.* I had to tread carefully. She could be triggered. Neoma could be jumpy when triggered.

I asked in as innocuous way as possible, 'Are you all right?'

'Didn't you get my text?' Her voice sounded croaky.

'I did. Why are you cancelling?'

'I told you. I don't need you anymore.'

That stung a little more than it should have.

I pushed past the rejection sting, to say, 'Neoma, what's going on?'

She lifted her hands in a defensive gesture. 'Please, leave.'

'Why?'

'I ... can't.'

'You can't what?'

'Nothing.'

'You know you can tell me anything.'

'It's not important.'

'What isn't?' She looked down, refusing to catch my gaze. 'Please, Neoma. This is the one time I'm begging you to talk to me.'

She shook her head as my instincts told me to hold my ground. There was something I was missing. I could almost feel it. It felt as if I reached out, I could touch the answer. What wasn't she saying?

In a too controlled tone, she said, 'I wish you every happiness, Emerson. I hope you and your new girlfriend are happy. I should get−−'

'Girlfriend?' She looked up at me, apparently catching the confused tone in my voice. 'What do you mean by "girlfriend"?'

'Well, your ... whatever she was. Anyway, I need to−−'

'Hang on.' I rubbed my head, trying to work out what was going on. 'Are you talking about Rose?'

She waved her hands in front of her face. 'I don't want to know the details. I need to go now.' She took a step back.

'Rose is my ghost writer.'

She paused. 'What?'

'She's my ghost writer.'

'Your ghost writer?'

'Yes.'

'She's not your girlfriend?'

'No.'

'She's not ... a one-night stand?'

Why did she want to know that? An instinct inside me said my answer was important.

'No.'

She seemed relieved.

That made me elaborate, 'It's been a while since I've had a relationship and the last time I slept with someone was only so I could forget ...' I trailed off when I realised what I'd almost confessed. I pressed my lips together, forcing myself to remain silent.

In a softened voice, Neoma asked, 'To forget what?'

I shook my head. 'Can we get back to why––'

She cut me off, saying, 'What do you want to forget, Emerson?'

Those words. So similar to what Sil had said to me in one of our sessions. *Why do you want to forget, Emerson?* A rush of memories invaded, mixing and merging into a confusing collage. Hostages. How to save them? No phone. No computer. No escape. A gun. *Bang.* The air in my lungs grew cold and heavy. I inhaled to lighten it, but it didn't work. I inhaled again. My chest squeezed, cutting off even more air flow.

Neoma's hand came to my arm as she said, 'Can you look at me?'

I hadn't realised I wasn't. I looked towards her.

Her forehead wrinkled in concern, 'I think you should come inside and sit down.'

Before I could say anything, she pulled me inside and, with a gentle touch, made me sit on a chair in her lounge room.

'I need you to look at the wall clock and tell me what time it is.'

My gaze searched the room for the clock. When I found it, I heard my raw voice say, 'One o'clock.'

The psychologist in me now acknowledged she was using my techniques––having me focus on her, getting me to move, asking a question my logical brain had to answer––as she had during my panic attack. She didn't need me anymore. The student had surpassed the master. She was right to have cancelled.

She pulled me from the conclusion, saying, 'Look at me again.'

I did.

She studied my face a moment, then said, 'Are you here with me?'

I nodded. 'I'm here with you, Neoma Seoma Alban.'

That made her smile. 'And, I'm here with you, Emerson ... I don't know your middle name ... Novak.'

I grinned. 'Jason.'

'Your middle name is Jason? Like Jason and the Argonauts?'

I nodded at her connection of my name to the Greek myth. Again, had she done that on purpose to get me thinking?

'Emerson Jason Novak. I like the sound of it.'

'Thank you.'

She smiled and brought her attention to me. It felt so good to see her happy and not trying to get rid of me.

Too soon, she looked away, and asked, 'Would you like a drink? Of water, to be clear.'

I grinned. 'Yes, please.'

My throat felt dry and sounded croaky.

As she turned from me, she gave my shoulder a comforting pat. I became too aware of the space where her hand had been when she left my side. *What's that about?* She returned a short time later with two glasses and handed one to me. I accepted the glass and took a sip while she sat beside me on the couch with her own drink. While she took a sip, she tried to make it look like she wasn't watching me from the corner of her eye, but I could tell she was.

'I really am all right. You can stop worrying.'

She hesitated, then, in a gentle tone, said, 'You don't have to tell me anything you don't want to tell me, but as someone who has told her story to someone recently, I can tell you it helps when it's the right time with the right person.'

I shook my head. 'This is different.'

'It always is when it's happened to you.'

I nodded because she was right.

'So?'

I exhaled.

Then told her the whole story.

I'd been stuck in the filing cabinet room for what had felt like days when Marshall had come in, drawn his gun, and been shot in the shoulder. From there, it had happened fast. Harry had rushed at the gunman, who had fired again. Thankfully, the bullet had hit the wall. At that point, the first hostage––I now knew his name was Bill–– joined in. The gunman was strong, and good at hand-to-hand combat. He defended himself against Bill and Harry's attacks with ease, but also dropped the gun. That was when a surge of energy had passed through me, and I'd known what to do. I'd run to the emergency exit and pushed it open. The alarm had sounded. Startled, the gunman had run. Simple fight or flight response. Self-preservation in its rawest form.

With the gunman gone, I felt like I was watching myself from somewhere outside of my body––deperson-alisation––when I acted next. I locked the emergency door again, then opened the filing room door and darted out to help Harry, Marshall, and Bill get up and inside the filing room with me. Once we were safely inside, I'd asked whether someone had a mobile and had used it––Harry's, I think––to call the onsite police. The gunman, whose name I still refused to mention, had been found a short distance away.

Once I finished telling Neoma my story, I took a long drink of water.

Neoma waited, then said, 'Is that why you got the bravery award?'

I looked at her. 'How did you know about that?'

'I may have done an internet search. You deserve the award. What you did was brave and courageous.'

I looked down. 'It doesn't feel that way sometimes.'

'Why not?'

'I didn't *do* anything, not until the last moment. Up

until then, I was an emotional, irrational ... coward.' The word made me cringe.

'You *weren't* a coward, Emerson. From what you've said, you were trying to figure out ways to help. Getting emotional doesn't make you a coward or irrational. Emotion helped you to remain hidden until you could help the others. You got them all out. They might have all been shot without you doing what you did. Your "irrational emotions" kept you and everyone else alive.'

Emotion had saved me and everyone else. All this time I had been so focused on shutting down my emotions, and the therapeutic benefits of 'logic,' that I'd missed the power of emotion. Neoma had helped bring that out in me. It was time I caught up with the benefits of 'feeling feelings' properly.

When I glanced over at her, I felt my eyes tear up.

Her face showed compassion as she asked, 'Would you like a hug?'

I nodded. She came close and wrapped her arms around me. This time, I let my arms come up and envelop her back. Relief washed away my tears.

After a moment, she pulled away. 'You okay?'

'Yes.'

She hesitated, then said, 'Is that why you use the screen in your sessions? Because it makes you feel safe, like you did hiding in that room?'

Sil had often made similar comments. Were they right? Had I subconsciously recreated trauma response elements? I'd long-believed I'd used the screen to stop myself from getting emotionally attached, and to keep my clients feeling safe. There was likely an element of that.

But, 'repetition compulsion' was a well-known Freudian psychoanalytical phenomenon, as were the lingering effects of trauma, though updated since Freud's time. Had I repeated the elements that had made *me* feel safe that day? *It's true.* My mind blasted forward with several instant decisions: no more screens in therapy; no more avoiding emotions … and no more ritual. It had taken Neoma to show me what real reconnection was about. Sometimes, it was messy, illogical, and even emotional. Here I was believing I'd been the 'expert' all this time. I almost laughed.

To her, I conceded, 'I think you might be right.'

In the silence, another insight came to me. *The one-night stands.* Was that another thing Sil had been right about? *Ugh.* Once this talk was over, I owed my ex-psychologist an apology phone call. But for now, something more pressing nudged at the back of my mind and demanded answers …

Chapter Forty Five

Neoma

Emerson asked, 'Can we go back to what you were talking about when I first arrived?'

Oh, no. This was not good.

'Do we have to?

'Yes. Why did you cancel our meetings? The real reason.'

'It's stupid.'

'Tell me anyway.'

'It's embarrassing.'

'I think we've both done enough embarrassing things in front of each other that one more won't make a difference at this point.'

'Says the man who doesn't have to be humiliated by the confession.'

'Tell me anyway. Please?'

I exhaled, and felt my cheeks get hot, so I looked away when I spoke, 'When I saw you with Rose, I might have gotten a teensy bit ... jealous.'

'Jealous? I'm confused ... aren't you dating Raj?'

'No.'

'You're not?'

I shook my head. 'I'm not dating anyone.'

'I'm not dating anyone, either.'

My chest thumped with that confession. Was it possible we could ... a second before I could finish the thought, Emerson jumped up from the chair.

Turning his back on me, he said, 'I should go.'

'But––'

'Thanks again for your help. I think you're right about cancelling the sessions. You don't need me anymore. Goodbye, Neoma.'

Without looking back, he walked out of Cara's house.

What. The. Heck. Was. That?

I frowned. *Maybe it's for the best?* He had been my therapist, after all. It might have gotten sticky. Except, he hadn't been my therapist at first. He'd been *Water Guy.* I shook my head, trying to stop the overthinking. None of this mattered. It was a good thing I'd ended the sessions. This way, I wouldn't have to see him again and would soon forget about him. Along with whatever the lump in my chest meant.

Chapter Forty Six

Emerson

My heart pounded in a clichéd panic as I jabbed at Sil's name on my phone that I'd placed in the car's phone stand and drove away from Neoma. The ring tone echoed through the phone's speaker.

'Come on, come on. Answer.'

The ring tone filtered through the line again. *Just great.* The one time he didn't want to speak to me was the one time I did. Giving up, I hung up and drove towards his office. I pulled to a screeching stop in a car park outside sooner than was legally allowed. Inside, his receptionist was missing. She must have been on a break. Rushing to his closed office door, I pounded, desperate to talk to him now.

'Sil? Sil? Sil!'

The door opened and Sil's concerned tone matched the look on his face when he said, 'What's wrong?'

'We need to talk.' I barged past him into his office. That's when noticed the person sitting in the room. *Shit*. I'd interrupted a session. That's why Sil hadn't answered the phone. I spun and faced Sil, who had followed after me. 'I'm sorry, I'll––'

'It's fine. We were finishing up here, anyway. Weren't we, Geno?'

The man nodded his head.

To me, Sil said, 'Grab a seat. I'll only be a minute.'

My ex-psychologist directed Geno out to the waiting room, then returned a few moments later. By that time, I'd calmed down enough to sit down. Sil closed the door then walked, calmly––I still don't know how he managed that in the midst of a crisis––towards me.

He sat on the chair opposite me and caught my gaze. 'Take a breath, Emerson.'

I closed my eyes and obeyed. He guided me through a few more breaths until I'd somewhat calmed down.

'Open your eyes and tell me what happened.'

I ran a hand down my face. 'I don't even know where to start.'

'From the beginning.'

'Neoma cancelled our meetings.'

'Why?'

'She said she doesn't need to see me anymore.'

'That's great news, isn't it? The therapy is working for her.'

'Yes.'

'Then, why does it bother you?'

'It doesn't, well, it does a little, but, no, it's not that. Not really. It's more because ... Neoma also hinted that she has feelings for me.'

'After she cancelled your meetings?'

'Yes.'

'How did she hint at having feelings for you?'

'She said she got jealous when she saw me with my ghost writer.'

'*After* she cancelled your meetings?'

Why was he being repetitive?

'Yes.'

'I see.'

'I'm glad you do because I sure as hell don't.'

'What are you worried about?'

'I don't know what to do.'

'What do you want to do?'

'If I knew that, I wouldn't be here.'

'Do you have feelings for Neoma?'

'Of course not. She's a client.'

'No, she's not. You said she called off your meetings.'

Ah, that's why he kept asking about the meetings.

'Well, she, yes, but ...'

My thoughts trailed off as another part of my brain took over. I thought back over the previous months. Moments that had seemed innocuous to me flooded my thoughts. First, the way it had bothered me not to know her story, when it had never bothered me before. Feeling like she had reignited my passion for psychology. The times I'd thought about her being 'pretty'. The urge to know more about her. The looks between Mum and Dad during our dinner together. Feeling nauseous––no, feeling *jealous*––when Neoma had been discussing Raj. Wanting to physically comfort her when she was upset. Kicking her door down. The other kicker: feeling bothered by other men checking her out at her work. Now I was looking at these snippets as a complete story, a sudden insight exploded in my head.

I jumped up from my seat. 'Shit. I think I have feelings for Neoma. I've got to go back and tell her.'

Sil put out a hand to stop me. 'You can't do that yet, Emerson.'

I was about to argue, when my mind locked on one word. 'Did you say *yet?*'

'Yes.'

'I don't understand.'

'Sit down and I'll explain.' Once seated, he continued, 'You can't be with her yet. However, there is a definite grey area here that we can work with.'

'What do you mean?'

'Considering you're not technically a psychologist anymore, and she isn't technically your client anymore, and she hasn't technically admitted to having feelings for you, and vice versa, I think after a decent amount of time has passed, say a year, with no contact, you could date her with less moral, ethical, and unbalanced power dynamics than if you rushed straight into it now. You can always continue to see your therapist to mitigate those problems if you do decide to go ahead with a relationship after the year has passed as well.'

It was definitely an option.

Another question came to me then. 'I'm curious. Why do you support me being with Neoma?'

'She has opened you up, Emerson. You're ready for proper recovery now, because of her. I've been nagging you for years to see a therapist. She comes into the picture, and you call me to give you the name of a therapist within two months.'

'You're right.'

'In that case, will you take more advice if I give it to you?'

'Yes.'

'Tell her how you feel, talk about the potential conflicts, then leave each other alone for a year, then see what happens. Absolutely no physical or other contact before then. If it's meant to be, the absence will strengthen your feelings.'

'Your advice is "absence makes the heart grow fonder"?'

He shrugged. 'Sometimes, the old sayings are the best.'

Unfortunately, the old-fashioned part of me agreed. The problem was: how could I broach this with Neoma? What if she didn't agree? What if she didn't want to wait for me? What if the power and ethical issues were too much for her? What if I had jumped to conclusions and she didn't feel anything for me? What if this was transference on her part? Wouldn't be the first time a client thought they had feelings for their therapist. *What about countertransference.* I frowned. Therapists falling for their clients was also a thing.

'What if this is transference and countertransference?'

Sil smiled. 'Guess what the time apart will do?'

'Show us if that's what this is.'

'Precisely. It works on several levels. But, you'll both

need to do some intensive therapy during the time apart as well.'

'I know.'

For the first time in years, I paid attention to the ache in my chest and didn't try to convince myself it meant nothing. Instead, I drew in a breath, and said, 'I need to go talk with Neoma.'

Chapter Forty Seven

Neoma

MARCH, four months later.

From the corner of my eye, I watched mum wrap a platter of finger sandwiches with cling wrap. After Emerson and I had spoken on that bizarre day four months ago, I'd felt brave enough to call her. We'd met up, and she'd been sincere in her apology. Since then, there hadn't been a single derogatory word about the attack from her lips. We'd also agreed to go to counselling together, and things between us had improved. There was still some progress to make, but it was a start.

I'd also started seeing a new counsellor. She wasn't as good as Emerson, but she was trauma-centred with some unorthodox qualities in her approach, so it was something. I'd need to be prepared for the unique challenges a change in my relationship with Emerson could create and she was helping with that, too. A loud knock on Cara's front door pulled me from my thoughts, and the hot party food I was organising. My heart jolted with the hope it was Emerson, here for my birthday party. That hope deflated when I recalled our no contact agreement.

I turned to mum, and said, 'I'll get it.'

When I opened the front door, several of my old friends greeted me. They rushed inside and enveloped me in hugs, bringing the warmth of the bright, cloudless day with them. I did everything I could to hide the hint of disappointment that hit me in the chest. It had been difficult not to see, talk to, or contact Emerson, but I'd caught the occasional glimpse of him on TV or the news. My boss had not asked me to edit his book, nor did I ask to be given the task. *No contact.* Still, it made me think of him whenever I saw my co-worker editing his book.

Sometimes, doubts plagued me. Had Emerson moved on? After all, four months could be a long time. I'd casually dated––we'd agreed we could date in the absence, because it was another way to test whether what we felt for each other was real––but nobody had interested me beyond a couple of booty calls. We still had eight months to go. The silence was almost like torture.

I wasn't allowed to wallow in my doubts any further because Cara took that moment to come out to the entry and say, 'All right, ladies. Let's get this party started!'

Epilogue

Neoma's Journal
Entry #159

I'm here. Sitting on the assigned seats on the promenade overlooking Sydney Harbour. It's getting dark and strangers are strolling around; some are getting close to me, and I feel fine about that. How different from twelve months ago! Lights from a couple of boats are blinking at me from across the water, almost like they are in on some shared secret. Is that a good sign or a bad one? Even though I've done several breathing and grounding exercises to prepare myself, I still feel tight (in my chest) and nauseous (below my diaphragm). I know it's a positive step for me to be this conscious of the way my body feels, but that doesn't mean my mind accepts it.

Thank goodness I've gotten into the habit of taking my journal everywhere. Writing in it gives me a sense of security.

Probably because it reminds me of Emerson. Ah, writing his name makes me feel more nervous. Oh, God. What if he doesn't come? No. He will. I know it sounds crazy—though both Mum and Cara said they trusted my intuition—but this is the first time I have felt so certain about anything in a long time. My body feels it, too. It's buzzing with the possibilities. Yes, the nausea and tightness are lingering, but that's nerves, and I'd say most people would feel nervous in this situation. Wouldn't they?

I mean, it's possible he won't come.

I need to take a break.

My head is starting to spin ...

Okay. That's better. I've taken more slow breaths, given my arms a shake, and swayed my upper body from side to side to shift as much anxiety as I can (got some funny looks, but who cares?). Now I can refocus and move the jumbled words from my mind, through my fingers, and onto the page. Unedited. That's still hard. Even after a year of practice. In some ways, the time has passed as fast as a blink; in other ways, it's lagged as slow as Cara's scooter on a good day. Speaking of slowness, how much longer until he gets here? My watch says 7pm. He shouldn't be far away.

Aah! What am I doing? This is insane. It's been a year. He's semi-famous now. Gorgeous models must be throwing themselves at him every day. He's not going to come back for me.

So what if he doesn't? Ha! I shrugged at that question. If he doesn't show, then Emerson's not the only fish in Sydney Harbour, is he? I'll be fine, whatever happens. I have been fine this past year. Better than I was for the six months before I met him. It will be his loss more than mine. I'm smiling now because I can feel the truth of that in my body. The tightness has gone. Only a touch of anxious nausea remains. I really have come a long way. My confidence is back. Finally. When I think about the events that brought me here, it's hard to believe I am the same woman who first met Emerson ...

'Neoma?'

My heart slammed in my chest as I whipped my head around. It's him. *Emerson. He's here.* I blinked. Is this real? He offered an uncertain smile, then stepped towards me. I saw a potted mini-sunflower in his hands. *I'll be the man with the sunflower.* That's what he'd said the last time we'd spoken, referencing the romance novel he'd assigned me. I couldn't stop the smile from spreading over my face as I popped my journal and pen back into my bag. Then, I ran to him. He bent to place the pot on the ground, then straightened and opened his arms just as I lunged at him. I sensed him smile as we hugged.

Against his chest, I whispered, 'You came.'

'So did you.' Obvious worry tinged his words.

'You thought I might not?'

'I had moments of doubt.'

'Same. I was worried you'd forget me.'

He pulled away to look at my face. 'How could I ever forget you? You changed my life.'

'You changed mine.'

He smiled, then said, 'I brought you something.'

He nodded at the pot on the ground.

I giggled. 'You remembered the sunflowers.'

'Do you like it?'

'It's beautiful.'

'Just like you.'

Aww. It was cheesy, but made my heart feel all oozy anyway. I gazed up into his eyes. As he stared back, it felt like the year slipped away and filled up with nothing but us. *He's here.* My heart fluttered with that realisation.

'Can I kiss you, Neoma?'

I nodded. How many times had I fantasised about our first kiss this past year? When he placed his lips against mine, warmth rushed through me, and I knew nothing would ever keep us apart again.

More from Serenade Publishing

Brigadier Station Series

By Sarah Williams:

The Brothers of Brigadier Station

The Sky over Brigadier Station

The Legacies of Brigadier Station

Christmas at Brigadier Station (An Outback Christmas Novella)

The Outback Governess (A Sweet Outback Novella)

Heart of the Hinterland Series

By Sarah Williams:

The Dairy Farmer's Daughter

Their Perfect Blend

Beyond the Barre

Primrose Series

By Tanya Renee

Prairie Sky

Prairie Nights

Prairie Fire

Prairie Hearts

The Spring of Love Series

By Virginia Taylor

Forever Delighted

Forever Amused

Forever Heartfelt

A New Page

By Aimee MacRae

It Happened in Paris

By Michelle Beesley

Middle Women

By Jack Garrety

Mim and Wiggy's Grand Adventure

By Jay McKenzie

A Dying Second Sun

By Peter A. Dowse

Winner Winner Chicken Dinner

By Sarah Jackson

Resurrection

By M H Austin

For more information visit:

www.serenadepublishing.com

About the Author

A.K. Leigh is a multi-published hybrid romance and non-fiction author, emerging trauma expert, identical triplet, and complex trauma survivor. Her PhD research identified and defined the post-trauma romance (PTR) subgenre, making her the world's leading expert on this subgenre, along with several innovative and new trauma theories. The Love Healer, written as part of her thesis, is an example of the PTR subgenre. She also holds a Masters degree in writing which resulted in the independent publication of her best-selling non-fiction title, The Romance Novel Formula.

Find out more at: www.fallinlovewithleigh.com

instagram.com/akleighauthor

Acknowledgments

This book would not have been possible without the support of my two brilliant PhD supervisors, Dr Nicole Anae and Dr Jan Cattoni. Their guidance, encouragement, and support pushed me forward throughout the roller coaster that is PhD research.

Likewise, without the funding of the Australian Government through the Research Training Program Living Stipend Scholarship, the completion of *The Love Healer* would have been much more difficult.

I would also like to thank Sarah Williams for her eager support of my manuscript and for bearing with me throughout the university release process. We got there in the end!

Most importantly, to the family, friends, and loved ones who stayed with me through the ups and downs of this journey: you are appreciated more than I can say. You are my "love healers".

I also wrote *The Love Healer* on the stolen lands of the Yuggerah people. I acknowledge the generational trauma that affects both this land and the lives of her original custodians.

Finally, it is my deepest hope that, one day, the need for trauma recovery journeys will be obsolete.

www.ingramcontent.com/pod-product-compliance
Lightning Source LLC
Chambersburg PA
CBHW072358110726
47909CB00003B/740